A Rag, a Bone and
a Hank of Hair

Other Oxford Children's Modern Classics

The Eagle of the Ninth
Rosemary Sutcliff

Outcast
Rosemary Sutcliff

The Silver Branch
Rosemary Sutcliff

The Lantern Bearers
Rosemary Sutcliff

Minnow on the Say
Philippa Pearce

Tom's Midnight Garden
Philippa Pearce

The Ship That Flew
Hilda Lewis

A Little Lower than the Angels
Geraldine McCaughrean

A Pack of Lies
Geraldine McCaughrean

Brother in the Land
Robert Swindells

Flambards
K. M. Peyton

The Edge of the Cloud
K. M. Peyton

Flambards in Summer
K. M. Peyton

Flambards Divided
K. M. Peyton

Wolf
Gillian Cross

The Great Elephant Chase
Gillian Cross

The Hounds of the Morrigan
Pat O'Shea

The Gauntlet
Ronald Welch

The Piemakers
Helen Cresswell

Jack Holborn
Leon Garfield

Mr Corbett's Ghost
Leon Garfield

Gumble's Yard
John Rowe Townsend

The Intruder
John Rowe Townsend

A Rag, a Bone and a Hank of Hair

It is the end of the twenty-second century and the birth-rate is starting to fall following a nuclear power leak. The government have begun to manufacture Reborns—new people made from dead ones. Brin has been chosen to help monitor the Reborn experiment and is sent to live with a family who have been recreated from 1940. For the experiment to work Brin must make sure that the members of this family never try to venture out into the real world—they would not survive or understand the twenty-second century—but the longer the experiment goes on, the harder it is to stop the Reborns discovering the truth about existence.

Nicholas Fisk is the very successful author of over forty books, including the science-fiction titles *Grinny, Mindbenders, On the Flip Side,* and *Trillions,* and has been described as 'the Huxley-Wyndham-Golding of children's literature'. Between leaving school and becoming a full-time writer, he worked as an assistant to a theatrical agent, a jazz musician, an actor, and a journalist, as well as spending four years in the RAF. Nicholas Fisk is married with four children, and lives in Hertfordshire.

A Rag, a Bone and a Hank of Hair

Nicholas Fisk

OXFORD
UNIVERSITY PRESS

OXFORD
UNIVERSITY PRESS

Great Clarendon Street, Oxford OX2 6DP

Oxford University Press is a department of the University of Oxford.
It furthers the University's objective of excellence in research, scholarship,
and education by publishing worldwide in

Oxford New York

Athens Auckland Bangkok Bogotá Buenos Aires Calcutta
Cape Town Chennai Dar es Salaam Delhi Florence Hong Kong Istanbul
Karachi Kuala Lumpur Madrid Melbourne Mexico City Mumbai
Nairobi Paris São Paulo Singapore Taipei Tokyo Toronto Warsaw

and associated companies in Berlin Ibadan

Oxford is a registered trade mark of Oxford University Press
in the UK and in certain other countries

British Library Cataloguing in Publication Data available

ISBN 0 19 271824 X

Typeset by AFS Image Setters Ltd, Glasgow
Printed and bound in Great Britain by
Biddles Ltd, Guildford and King's Lynn

The Chancellor who led Brin through the corridors was nobody important: just an elderly man with various bits of coloured ribbon on his white tunic to show how distinguished he was. Or had been. He was too old to matter now. Brin was young enough to matter.

The corridors were long, high-arched, and splendid. The tall windows were radiant and mellow with moving pictures, constantly changing, showing historical achievements of the western world. Brin wanted to slow down, to look at them properly—but the Chancellor shuffled on anxiously, towing Brin along. 'Quickly, young man!' he said, 'they're waiting for you! The Seniors are waiting!' Brin let himself be hurried, smiling at the humped old back and the gasping voice. After all, the Chancellor was old and useless. Brin was young and priceless.

'In there, boy!' said the Chancellor and opened the great doors. Before Brin was the Council Chamber of the Western Elect. In the Chamber were the Seniors of the Western Elect. They ruled the whole western world—one third and more of the planet Earth. They were important, yes: but they were all old.

The Chancellor gave Brin a nervous push towards a solitary white chair set in the middle of the great horseshoe curve of the Seniors' desk. Brin made the Sign of Politeness and sat down in the white chair. He did not ask permission to sit and he did not hurry as he settled himself. Comfortable, he stared at the Seniors. Silent, they stared at him.

The Chancellor—his voice shaking with respect and awe—announced Brin. 'Brin Tuptal,' he said, 'Young Citizen First Grade, 3/нм 160—'

'We know all that,' said one of the Seniors, peevishly. This Senior sat in the middle of the horseshoe desk: 'The senior Senior,' Brin said to himself. The Senior Elect. He had a long nose. He looked much older than he did on the viddy screens—but even on TV he looked old enough.

'Let the boy speak for himself,' said the Senior Elect. 'Well, Brin?'

'Well,' Brin replied, 'I am Brin Tuptal and I'm twelve. I am cleverer than most people.' He stared straight at the senior Senior, who scratched his nose, apparently uninterested. Brin shifted his stare to a brown-faced Senior; a woman. She looked Indian, her hair was blue-black and her skin brown. She smiled at Brin. To her right was another woman Senior, a horse-faced elderly woman. She too smiled at Brin, showing long white horsy teeth.

'What is your IQ, Brin?' she asked.

'180 when I was tested by the Broningen rating. But it may be even higher on other ratings. Probably I'm a genius.'

Brin thought he heard the Senior Elect mutter, 'Probably not,'—but no doubt Brin misheard. Old people were not rude to young people.

Brin looked around him. Domed glass above him: a clear curve, showing the blue sky. It would not rain until Thursday. Today was Tuesday. He looked at the white, curved walls of the Council Chamber—the electronic displays, the illuminated, moving maps, the always changing readouts. Gadgets. But there were no gadgets on the Seniors' desk. The nine Seniors made a bleak, bare picture in their white robes. Their faces supplied the only

2

colours. One almost black, one brown, one golden yellow, the rest white.

'Well?' said the Senior Elect. 'Go on. Don't waste time. Talk.' There was no respect in his voice, no politeness. Brin was surprised. He shrugged and said, 'Talk about what?' He looked from face to face and began to recite, '*You* are the Senior in charge of internal social affairs. And *you*, you're the Senior in charge of food production—agriculture, fisheries, hydroponics, climate—' He rolled off the words glibly, sure of himself, until the Senior Elect said, 'Enough. Talk about yourself. And don't be childish.'

Childish! Brin was shocked. He was seldom spoken to roughly. In Babyland, the state had taken care of him, gently. In Primary, it had been all Finger-painting and Experiences and Wonder of Living. Never a cross word, never a frown. And now he was twelve, and rare, and important—and grown-up people were being rude to him.

The horse-faced Senior prompted him. 'You were saying you were a clever person—a person of high intelligence. Tell us more, Brin.' She smiled invitingly, arching her long neck to one side.

Brin said, 'I knew I was different from the others. Even in Primary. They messed about and played stupid games all the time. I learned things. Lots of things.'

'What sort of things?' said the Senior with the only face Brin liked—the golden-faced Chinese-looking woman.

'Anything,' Brin told her. 'Everything.'

The Chinese-looking Senior laughed. 'Everything?' she said. 'You learned everything?' Brin was not sure that her laughter was kind.

'I didn't mean that, you know I didn't mean that!' he said. He could hear himself getting rattled, hear his own voice rising to too high a pitch. 'I don't mean that I *know* everything, just that—'

'Get on, get on,' said the Senior Elect. Other Seniors were smiling privately. Brin was confused. He was not used to being laughed at. Sulkily, he refused to speak.

At last, the Chinese-looking Senior said, 'So you learn very fast, do you?'

'Very fast indeed. Faster than anyone I know. Faster than anyone in the Teens. I'm twelve, but they've put me with the Teens because I know so much. I'm brilliant, they say I'm brilliant. I can learn anything—'

'Oh dear, oh dear, he won't do,' said the Senior Elect. 'Swell-headed little ape,' he seemed to add, in a mutter. (But that, Brin knew, was impossible. No one dared be that rude to a young person.) The black Senior yawned. The horse-faced Senior looked over Brin's head. Brin was not used to being ignored.

The black-faced Senior suddenly snapped, 'What's Politics? What's Ecology? Quick!'

Brin jumped. He was almost frightened. No one ever spoke to him like that. 'P-politics,' he began, hearing himself stutter, 'is the art and science of ruling people—of ruling *peoples*—'

'Well, well,' sneered the Senior Elect. 'Try Ecology.'

'Ecology is the science of preserving the place we live in—seeing to the environment and—'

The Senior Elect cut him short. 'What are *Reborns*?' he demanded.

Brin gaped at him. Had he heard rightly? Had he really said '*Reborns*'?

'Reborns, Reborns, *Reborns*!' said the Senior, leaning forward over the table. 'Tell us about them!'

'But they mustn't be talked about!—'

'Oh yes they must. Here and now. Quickly!'

'Reborns are manufactured people,' Brin began. 'New people made out of old people.'

'How?' said the Senior Elect.

'There could be several ways, I don't know if—'

'You told us a moment ago that you'd learned everything,' said a youngish Senior, a woman, who had not spoken before. She had big eyes and a small mouth, a tight little mouth, but now it was open, showing small white teeth. The round eyes were staring at him. He was not used to being stared at.

Brin sat back in his chair, feeling his back meet the soft pad. He settled himself deliberately: braced his mind and body and said, 'You're all rude and stupid. You're rude to me. You are the Seniors but you behave like bad children. I'd like to go now.'

'*That's* better!' said the Senior Elect, rubbing his narrow hands. He actually smiled. 'Go on, boy. Tell us about Reborns.'

'Only if you obey the Rules of Politeness,' said Brin, making the Sign of Politeness used by all Westerners when a discussion goes wrong and a quarrel might start—a touch of the fingers to the head, where the brain is; then to the heart. It was an old sign, an ancient sign, the Christians had used something like it until a few centuries ago. You were supposed to reply to it.

Most of the Seniors made the sign back, but two of them didn't, probably deliberately. An insult! Brin got to his feet and prepared to leave.

The voice of the Senior Elect stopped him. The voice was gentle now, completely changed, soft and low and pleasant. 'Please sit down, Brin.' The Senior made the sign and Brin automatically replied. 'Tell us about the Reborns. Tell us what you know and don't know. We are on a friendly footing now—'

'We had to test you,' said the golden-faced woman.

5

'You see we have to try and find out if you are the right person to do the work we want done. But tell us about Reborns.' She smiled. Her face was charming.

Brin settled back in his chair and began.

'First,' he said, 'I'll tell you what I know—what people are saying, that is. Because we don't really know anything, only what you let us know. Anyhow . . .

'In the last century, there was an accident at the Euronuclear power plant. A leakage. After the accident, the birthrate began to fall. Many people who wanted to be parents could not have children. Children became very—very valuable, because there weren't enough of them. Of us. So we had to be taken care of. Educated carefully, brought up to be healthy and so on.

'Then,' he continued, 'the damage proved worse than anyone thought. The accident affected the whole world. There were less and less children. So the population of the world went down and down. And those stupid jokes started appearing—you know, "Robots Rule!"—all those jokes about the machines taking over our world when all the people were gone.'

' "Robots Rule!" ' said one of the Seniors; 'Very good!' The Senior Elect waved him silent and said, 'Go on, Brin.'

'Well, there had to be more people, far too few could be born naturally. So you Seniors started thinking about Reborns. And now everyone has heard rumours about them but nobody really knows what they'll be like, or what they are, or will be.'

'Do you know?' a Senior asked.

'I've looked the subject up. Genetics, DNA, genes, chromosomes, the elements of living things—'

'How do you think Reborns will be made?'

'Every part of every living thing,' Brin began,

concentrating hard and staring straight ahead of himself, 'contains its own recipe. A tiny bit of lettuce contains the recipe for the whole lettuce. Part of a fingernail contains the recipe for the whole fingernail. Scraps of bone and tissue from the flesh of a cat or dog contain the recipe for the whole animal—'

'Very well put!' said the Chinese-looking Senior, beaming.

'Excellent!' agreed the once-peevish Senior Elect. 'Go on.'

Brin continued, 'I suppose what you'd do is something like this: you'd get various scraps of tissue, bone, anything, and put them in a Genetic Recoder. And then in a sort of soup. With some electricity of course. You'd cook it up. And then you would have living matter, even a living human being. A new human just the same as the old one. A reborn human.'

'Right!' said the black Senior. 'Right, that is, in every way but one. You said, "That is what we would do." You should have said—"That is what we have done!"'

Brin said, 'You mean, the rumours are true? You have already made some Reborns?'

'Yes. Otherwise we would not have encouraged the rumours.'

'Are there many Reborns?'

'No—very, very few.'

'Are they—all right? Do they behave like real human beings?'

'They *are* real human beings. Not robots, or machines, or androids, or those delightful creatures in the old films—'

'You mean Frankenstein's monsters?' Brin said, 'with nuts and bolts sticking out of their necks and great big boots on?'

The Senior Elect, to Brin's astonishment, began to

7

chuckle. 'Well, well! Remarkable boy! Seen everything, knows everything. Even the ancient cinema films! Mind you, I never understood what the heavy boots were for. Slippers far more suitable—'

Brin grew impatient and interrupted. 'So you have solved the problem of repeopling the planet?' he said.

'Ah,' said the brown, Indian-looking Senior. She stroked her chin and stared at Brin.

'Ah,' said the other Seniors, looking at Brin and each other.

There was a silence until the black Senior's rich voice spoke, 'There are problems,' he said. 'Problems . . . ' The dark eyes in the broad, black powerful face fixed themselves on Brin's eyes: the big voice said, 'You are going to solve the problems, Brin!'

'This way,' said the black Senior, putting his heavy hand on Brin's shoulder and guiding him through a door in a long, bare corridor.

There was a guard at the door, a hard-faced woman in the usual one-piece uniform made of Adamant. You could see her determined face through the visor of her helmet and just about hear the whispering of her uniform's air-conditioning unit. Adamant lets nothing in—and nothing out: the unit had to do her body's breathing. *Fsss!* went the aircon unit, and each time Brin smelled the rather nasty perfume the woman wore.

The black Senior said, 'Brin, you ought to know my name. I am Tello, after Othello. Do you know who Othello was?'

Brin promptly answered, 'Othello, Moorish king—Moors were black. William Shakespeare tragedy, still performed—'

Tello chuckled and held up a big hand to silence Brin. 'All right,' he said. 'You know about Othello.'

The guard said, 'Prints, please.'

'You know me, Maisie!' laughed Tello, turning to the guard.

'I know I want your prints. Yours and his.'

'The boy hasn't got prints, he's just a . . . a boy—'

'Get away from here, then. You and the boy. Come back when you've got prints.' She put her hand on the Viper control on her belt. Tello backed away, laughing and protesting.

'All right, Maisie! Going quietly! Won't come back till we've both got prints!' They walked down the corridor, away from the door. Tello shook his head and smiled. 'She's a dragon, that one!'

'But she was rude! Almost violent!' Brin said, deeply shocked.

'Trained to be,' Tello said, contentedly.

'But I thought the whole *idea* of our society was—' Brin began, then gave up.

'Sweetness and light?' Tello said. 'No violence, no aggression?' He chuckled. 'Well, that's what you see. And Maisie is what you don't see. But she's there all the same.'

'But she wouldn't have used her Viper on you, would she?'

'Not on me! Perhaps on you. She knows me all right, of course—but though she has known me for years, she'd have had you smoking on the floor if we hadn't moved off!'

'Smoking?'

'When you get hit by a Viper, you burn. When you burn, you smoke.'

'What *is* a Viper?'

'The weapon in the suit. The weapon is the suit and the suit is the weapon. Maisie just occupies the weapon. She doesn't have to be strong—just strong-minded. And Maisie's that!'

Now they were in what seemed to be a Records office. The man behind the desk took Brin's hand and did things with it over bits of plastic and a little machine that hummed.

Brin paid no attention. He guessed, correctly, that the fingermarks and their chemistry were being recorded and registered and that when this was done he could put his prints on the coding panel of the door Maisie guarded. Then the door would be opened for him. He wondered what could be behind the door.

Something very important. Something as important as a Reborn? He could not ask such questions out loud so he kept still while the man behind the desk fussed about with computers and card machines and all the rest of it.

'Completed, sir,' the man said to Tello. (Sir! thought Brin. He had never heard the word used except in old films and TV programmes. The word had an old-fashioned ring to it. It must be wonderful to be a Senior and be called 'Sir'.)

Now the man was speaking to him, Brin. 'This is your card, sir,' he said. (Me a 'sir'! thought Brin.) 'You'll need to write down your code number—'

'I don't need to. I can remember it. I can remember any number you like—'

'Write it down, sir. Then sign your name underneath in your usual handwriting. Thank you. That is all.'

'Don't I get the card?'

'Certainly not! We keep the card, sir.'

Brin asked the man, 'What does it mean, all this? Does it mean I can go in anywhere—into all the doors in this place, past all the guards?'

'Oh no, sir. Nothing like that, sir. It means that you can print in—you may enter certain places—in the company of a Senior. But only when accompanied by a Senior.'

10

'What a lot of nonsense!' Brin burst out. 'I thought all this sort of thing had been done away with centuries ago!'

'Did you, sir?' said the man. 'Did you think that?' Coolly, he turned away and went back to his machines.

'Come on, boy,' said Tello. He began chuckling again as they walked back along the corridor. 'He's got a card,' the big, dark voice muttered and rumbled as they walked, 'He's got Coded Status, and a number, and he can actually *print in*—and he's grumbling!'

Brin, confused, said nothing.

At the guarded door, Maisie said, 'Prints, please.'

Tello put out his hand, first to a flat plate on Maisie's shoulder, then to a similar plate to the side of the door. A rose-pink light in the door lit and slowly faded.

'Now the boy.'

Brin imitated Tello's actions. Again the rose-pink light glowed and faded. The door opened.

They entered a small room closed by another door. They sat down. Tello was silent now and unsmiling. Brin fidgeted and at last said, 'Where am I going? What's going to happen?'

The second door opened and a pretty girl said, 'Tello, sir. And Brin. Please come in.'

They walked straight into November, 1940.

November, 1940, was badly lit, smelly, spacious, complicated, clumsy, dingy and noisy. The noises were small. A ticking clock, a dripping tap, a kitchen range whose grate went 'Grr-grr-TANG!' as the live coals dropped under the vibration of their footsteps, then gently clicked and murmured as the coals settled and burned anew.

'The 1940 Scenario, sir,' said the pretty girl, smiling brightly.

'The what?' said Brin. Only half of what he saw meant anything to him. That over there—that was a chair of some kind, obviously. But what kind? The girl, following his eyes, said, 'Wicker chair. Wicker is sort of sticks, things that grow. People collected them, twisted them, made them into chairs and so on.' She went to the chair and sat herself in it crisply, her neat trouser suit garish and wrong against the creaking yellowish wicker and faded floral cushion of the chair.

Tello said, 'Give him the guided tour, Madi.'

'Wouldn't you rather, sir? I mean, you are in charge . . . ?'

'You did the work. Tell him all about it.'

The girl called Madi said, 'Right. Do I call you Brin or Sir?'

'Brin.'

'Well, Brin, this is the kitchen, larder, and scullery of an old house in West London of 1940. There is an outside lavatory through that door, the "back door". You are standing in the kitchen. Facing the window, on that wall, you can see a *dresser*, with drawers and shelves to hold the plates and knives and forks and other things for cooking and serving food. That thing you are looking at shouldn't be on the dresser, it should be in one of the drawers. It's called an eggbeater and it works like this.' She took hold of the grey-and-silver ancient machine and whirled its handle. The beating blades whirred tinnily, the bent-tin cogwheels meshed and juddered.

'It could actually work!' said Brin. 'You could beat eggs with that thing!'

'It did work,' the girl said, putting it in a dresser drawer. 'It does work! Definitely beats eggs!' She smiled briefly at Brin and picked up the next exhibit, the clock. 'Alarm clock!' she announced, shaking it. It made sad tinny noises then picked up its ticking again, tick-tock, tick-tock. 'Tells the time,' said Madi, 'rings a bell to wake you up or get the food out of the cooker when it's done. OK?'

'What cooker?' said Brin, still amazed, but fascinated.

She showed him the cast-iron kitchen range and the other sort of cooker, the ugly grey-and-white gas one, with its brass taps. She showed him rolling pins and jelly moulds, tins of custard powder and a meat-safe made of wood and galvanized metal; flypapers and biscuits, shoe polish and scouring powders, coal and gelatine, mousetraps and flat-irons.

Brin drank it all in.

'You see, the scullery is where you take the dirty things to be washed up—there's the sink, there's the sink-tidy, and the little mop and brush for crockery, and soda (which is like detergents) and—Brin, are you sure you are remembering all this?'

'I'm sure,' he said.

'That's why we picked him,' said Tello, smiling happily from the creaking wicker armchair.

'I don't trust him!' the girl laughed. 'What's a Ewbank, Brin?'

He said, 'Carpet-sweeper. That wood-cased thing with rubber wheels and brushes inside.'

'Hoover?'

'Vacuum cleaner. Kept in that cupboard over there.'

'Skipper?'

'Sardines.'

'Main?'

'The name on that gas cooker.'

'Cherry Blossom?'

'Boot polish. But they wear shoes, not boots.'

The girl paused. 'He's good, sir,' she said to Tello. 'You picked the right boy! Now listen carefully. There is a lot to remember . . .'

Later, she questioned Brin. 'What is blancmange? Rinso? Methylated spirits? Lino? Stair-rod? Ice box? Lard? What's the difference between socks and stockings? Between coal and coke? Between shoes and slippers? Between high tea and tea-time tea?'

Brin got every answer right. When she said, 'November, 1940 . . . What is happening in the world?' he answered, 'World War Two has started and—' He told her at length.

'You're marvellous, Brin!' she said.

'No, I'm not. I can't answer some questions.'

'What questions?'

Brin put his hands on his hips, stared her in the face and said, 'Why am I here? What's it all for? What's a scenario?'

'Ah,' said Tello, 'I'll answer, Madi . . . '

'First,' Tello said, when Brin was sitting uncomfortably on a hard wooden kitchen chair covered with chipped cream paint, 'First, the word *Scenario*.

'A scenario is a setting for people, or actions, or both. It's like a stage-set—but also like a situation. Now, we need both. We need a *place* for certain characters to act out their play; we also need a *situation* in which those people will feel at home.'

'What people? What characters?'

'Come to that in a moment. You asked, ''Why am I here?'' You're here because you are the right person—the right age—and because you've got a wonderful memory, a huge ability to learn fast. You are here because you're probably the only person who could do the job.

'Then, Brin,' he continued, 'you asked, ''What's it all for?'' Well, that's easily answered. It's here for the Reborns.'

'The Reborns!'

'That's what I said. The Reborns. They are the central characters in the play, Brin. This Scenario was lovingly

14

put together by Madi for them. All these things—these wicker chairs and mousetraps and kitchen sinks and I-don't-know-whats—Madi had them reborn, found them, or had them made. Are you beginning to get it?'

Brin thought, and said, 'Of course! Yes! I see it! The Reborns are 1940 people, you've picked people from that period—and this is their home, the place where they'll feel at home—'

'That's it,' said Tello, smiling and leaning back in his creaky chair.

'But why bother with this Scenario? Why not bring them straight into our own time? Why go back in the past?'

Before Tello could answer, Brin said, 'No—wait—the past: why go back to the past for Reborns? Why go to all that trouble? Why not make Reborns from *proper* people— recently-dead people of our own time? Why go back to 1940?'

'Uh-uh!' said Tello. 'Think, Brin! You're not thinking! Think!'

Brin thought: and at last said, 'Oh. I see. I get it.'

'What do you get?'

'Well, it's a sort of catch, isn't it? Catch-question, catch-answer. The reason we need Reborns is, that our people, the real people, "proper" people, can't reproduce themselves any more. And if you made Reborns from Reborns, you'd only produce *more* people who couldn't breed: which would mean producing more Reborns. In fact, you'd be stuck with Reborns for the whole future of mankind!'

'You've got it,' Tello said. 'But I ask you again why 1940? Why not 1920, 1960, 1980? Why 1940 in particular?'

'The war?' Brin said. 'Has that got something to do with it?'

'Go on,' Tello said.

'The war . . . ' Brin muttered. 'Let's think . . . There was the blackout. And fear of bombs. And rationing and shortages—'

'Good lad!' Tello said. 'More.'

'Well, I suppose people led restricted lives. Like being in prison, almost. You were stuck in your home, once darkness fell, because there was no point in going out.'

'And there was no point in *wanting* to go out,' Tello said, continuing Brin's thoughts. 'Go out for what? For a meal? Well, you could, but restaurant meals weren't all that exciting. And children didn't go out on their own to restaurants. The cinema? Yes—but buses and trains stopped early, and there was the blackout to face and children weren't allowed into cinemas without an accompanying adult. So people stayed home. They expected to stay home. Which suits our Scenario nicely.'

'But you could have used a later period?' Brin asked.

'Perhaps. But probably not. By 1960 or 1980, children wanted all kinds of things—and got what they wanted! They expected freedoms and possessions and excitements. So later children wouldn't have done for us. They would almost certainly become impatient with the Scenario. We could condition our Reborns *not* to become impatient: but that wouldn't do either. Too much conditioning tampers with the natural being we want to observe.'

Brin interrupted. 'All right. But why bother with this Scenario? Why not bring the 1940 Reborns right into our own time, straight away?'

Tello said, 'Look, it's no good just dragging people out of their graves and putting them down in a completely new place and situation! The Scenario must fit. They must be put at ease. Otherwise, they might not be able to take it all in. They might be terrified, angry, shocked, anything. And worse than that—'

'Worse than that, we wouldn't be able to understand *them*?' Brin suggested.

'Right!' said Tello. 'We don't want to know what our Reborns might do or should do or could do: we want to know what they *do* do—how they behave in their own surroundings living life their own way. Only then can we find how to bring them "up to date"—how to help them fit in with our times, our lives. How to find them a place, if there *is* a place for them. Perhaps there isn't. Perhaps the jump from then to now is too much for anyone to make. We must find out. When we've learned all we need to learn about them, we can try different ways, perhaps. We can throw them in at the deep end, try mixing Reborns of different races and periods, try anything. But not at first . . . '

'And where,' Brin said, 'do I come in?'

'Oh, I didn't tell you, did I?' Tello said. 'The first Reborns were young people. People of your age or younger. People not too old to learn. We have had failures and successes . . . '

'So?' said Brin. He scratched his left armpit. It itched.

'So you're it!' Tello beamed. 'You're the host! You're the one who's going to live with them, share their lives, learn about them!'

Brin got up from the chair so fast that it fell over backwards. 'I'm not, you know!' he said. 'I'm going straight back home to my own life, with my own friends! I'll live in my own time and learn the things I want to learn!'

Tello smiled more broadly than ever and said, 'You'll do as you're told, boy.'

Madi, behind him, picked up the fallen chair and gently pushed Brin's shoulders until he sat in it. 'We've all got a duty, Brin,' she said, smiling prettily at him. 'We have to do our duty.'

'I won't do mine,' Brin said.

Tello stood up, towering over Brin. 'Don't be silly, Brin,' he said, in his easy velvety bass. 'I told you: you're *it*. And when one of the Seniors tells you a thing like that, you just simply say "Yes, sir".' The big, dark face was still smiling, still pleasant, still likeable. But Brin could also see something else in it, something hard as rock: something that made Tello a Senior and himself a Junior.

'Yes, sir . . . ?' Tello prompted.

'I suppose so,' Brin muttered. 'Yes, sir.'

The ugly old alarm clock on the dresser went BRRRRRRR! and Madi said, 'You've got quarter of an hour, Brin. There's a lot to learn in that time.'

'And at the end of that time?' Brin asked, miserably.

'*They* arrive,' Madi said.

But it took Brin only ten minutes to learn all he needed to know: to find out about knife sharpeners, can openers, ink, dish mops, draining boards, bread bins, coffee percolators, the importance of cups of tea and the cat's bowl of milk. And to change into his 1940 clothes—long itchy socks, heavy shoes, flannel shorts, shirt and a stupid thing called a tie. He kept his own underclothes.

He had plenty of time to ask the questions that really interested him. 'Is this all there was, Madi? Just these rooms?'

'No. This is just a part of a house of that period. Many people in those days lived in big houses with lots of rooms. Above this set of rooms there should be other rooms—bedrooms, bathrooms, sitting-rooms, an attic. Beside it, there'd be a dining-room and a room called the drawing-room. There's a garden outside, you can see a little bit of it through the window.'

'But the Reborns will want to go to those other rooms.'

'No they won't. We made the Reborns. We programmed them—conditioned them to expect and accept what we offer them.'

'But couldn't you have offered them a bit more than this?' Brin asked, looking round the dingy room.

Madi rolled her eyes and said, 'If you knew the trouble, the effort, the research, that went into getting just this bit done! That carpet over there—that little thing in front of the range—that's a Reborn! It's made of cotton and wool, natural fibres; we had to reborn it from a little old tuft we found—'

'But what about the other things?'

'We had to find them. Or make them. And that's not all, we had to "antique" them—give the appearance of being old and used. That aluminium coffee percolator, all stained at the bottom—'

'It's incredible!'

'Incredible. Yet nothing compared with making the Reborns themselves.'

'Tell me about making them,' Brin said.

'There's not time. And even if there was, I don't know enough. I'm just an Effects worker, I'd nothing to do with the *people* side. And the people will be here any minute now.'

'I wish you'd tell me more about them.'

'There's Mavis, nine. And Brian, eleven. Brother and sister. Wait and see.'

'You could at least tell me if they're bigger or smaller than me—if they're clever or stupid—if—' Madi put a finger to her lips, swung the whole dresser outwards like a great door, stepped behind it and swung the dresser shut.

Brin caught her whispered words. 'They're here! Ready?'

'I suppose so,' Brin muttered.

The door opened and Mavis and Brian came in.

Mavis called 'Coooee,' then stopped short, hand to mouth, when she saw Brin. 'Oh! I'd forgotten about you!' she said.

She extended her right hand. Brin took it and shook it. He looked at her eagerly, inspecting her, but she did not meet his eyes. She just shook his hand, limply, and said, 'I'm Mavis. Well, you know that . . . Brian, Brin's here!' Then, remembering her manners, she said, 'How do you do,' and looked him properly in the eye for the first time.

She was as tall as Brin although she was only nine. Her head seemed small to Brin, but shapely and rather pretty. Her hair, cut short, was not pretty—not quite clean, and held in place with—what was the word?—a *slide*, a little imitation tortoiseshell clip. She saw his eyes look at the slide and her ink-stained fingers flew to it and unclipped it. 'School rule, we've jolly well got to wear them!' she said and then grinned awkwardly.

Brian came in.

To Brin, he seemed big, raw, and animal. His knees were grey with dirt, red with a cut, white where the skin had been scraped. One of his teeth was crooked. There was ink on one ear. He put out his strong, grubby hand.

Brian said, 'I'm Brian. How do you do!' then stared at Brin, with his mouth half open in an awkward grin. Brin glimpsed bits of metal in Brian's back teeth. Stoppers? No, *stoppings*.

Brin realized he was being rude by looking so openly at Brian. You were supposed to be shy, it was bad manners to stare. He wondered whether he ought to say something. He began to say, 'How do you—' when Brian leapt away from him and shouted, 'Super! Bananas!' He grabbed a banana, peeled it and then stopped. 'Gosh,' he said. 'There's only two. Do you want one, Brin?'

Mavis said, 'Ladies first, thank you!' and took the banana from her brother. She began to eat it.

'Well, I like that!' Brian exploded.

Brin said, 'I don't want a banana. You have the other one . . .'

Brian said, 'We could split it.' He paused, then said, '*Banana split*, get it? Ho, ho!'

Brin did not know what he meant so he laughed. Mavis, her banana nearly finished, imitated her brother's laugh, and said, 'Funny joke. Tee-hee.'

'No need to get sarky,' Brian said angrily.

'Well, I *mean*,' Mavis said scornfully, imitating Brian's laugh. 'Ho, ho, нo! You and your Ho, ho, нo! Is that all they teach you at that school?'

'Nark it!' Brian said, and stuffed the banana into his mouth, scowling.

Brin watched and listened. The sky was darkening fast outside, turning prison-grey. The room suddenly blazed with harsh light from a single, central bulb as Mavis flicked the switch by the door. Every ugly detail was revealed by the light.

Brin looked and despaired.

Yet half an hour later, he was happy.

The happiness began when Brian had kicked his satchel into the corner, loosened his school tie, thrown his cap at the dresser and made himself comfortable. He said, 'Let's have soldier's toast! With Marmite!'

Brian and Mavis crouched by the kitchen range, holding buttered bread over the glowing coal until the underside scorched. Brin watched amazed. The half-burnt bread and butter was smeared with brown stuff from a little dark pot with a paper label on it showing a picture of a different little brown pot: this was obviously Marmite.

Mavis said, 'Here you are, Brin! More in a sec!' and pushed the burned, smeared bread at him on a long wire fork. He wondered what to do with the reeking square of—food?—and delayed until Mavis and Brian did something.

It *was* food: they ate it.

He tried a corner of his piece of soldier's toast. Then a larger bite. Then an enormous bite.

Salty, buttery, crunchy yet soft. Delicious!

'Encore!' Brian said.

'Encore!' said Brin, hoping the word would mean another slice of soldier's toast and Marmite.

It did. And a third, this time with tea from a brown pot.

'Super!' Brin said, and meant it.

'What did you make of it, your first day?' Madi asked. She had a Squeaker on a gold chain round her neck, so Brin knew that their conversation was being recorded. Later, the little Squeaker, no bigger than a brooch, would be slotted into a Scripta. The tiny wire spool inside would squeak its record of the conversation: the Scripta would turn sounds into written words for microfilm projection, so that the words could be read; or for coding and filing in The Memory Bank; or anything else.

Squeakers were among the few things that made Brin nervous. He knew why. It was his vanity. He was proud of his cleverness. He hated to say—and have recorded—anything foolish or imprecise. He knew that his Squeaker record would be studied by the Seniors. So he answered Madi grudgingly and carefully. 'It was all right,' he said.

'All right?' Madi smiled brightly at him, demanding more.

'All right. But difficult. They speak a different language. They never say what they mean. They sort of . . . make a sketch of their thoughts and intentions. They hide everything behind catchphrases and acting. They are not like us.'

'I know what you mean,' Madi said. 'I was watching and listening. Go on, Brin.'

'Well, it's hard to know what they're really thinking, what they're really like,' Brin said, lamely.

'Yes. I've made a list of some of their words and phrases.' She squeezed the Squeaker to change track. Its little voice squeaked, *'Barmy. Nuts. Super. Gosh. I say. Soppy. Ridic. Nark it. Gertcher.'* It sang, in a mocking voice, *'The roses round the door . . . make me love mother more'* (Brian sang that when Mavis had said something 'soppy'). It sang, *'I like a nice cup of tea in the morning'* (that was when Mavis put the kettle on). It repeated, *'How do you do. Thank your mother for the rabbit, Ain't it grand to be bloomin' well dead; and Any rags, bottles or bones.'*

'What do you make of all that, Brin?'

'I don't know. Catchphrases. From the wireless, the radio. They have it on a lot, in the background.'

'They had gramophone records too,' she said. 'No telly, of course. But cinema films. So Mavis and Brian were quoting what they heard on the radio and on gramophone records.'

Brin asked, 'But why do they never seem to speak any of their own thoughts?'

'Perhaps they are shy. Perhaps they hide behind the catchphrases.'

'Or perhaps,' Brin said, 'they have nothing to say. Nothing worth saying . . . '

After a pause, Madi said, 'Does that mean you don't think very much of them?'

'I don't know,' Brin said, confused. 'You shouldn't ask that after just one meeting. It's too early to tell.'

'But we've got to find out, Brin. As quickly as possible. I'm sure you know why?'

'Well, it's obvious. We've got to know whether people of this quality are worthwhile. Whether the breed is good enough—'

' "Silk purse, sow's ear",' Madi said. 'We've got to know which.'

'Well, I don't know which. It's too early to say.'

'Are they as intelligent as you?' Madi asked.

'No.'

'Are they as well educated as you?'

'No. How could they be? They belong to the old days. Nearly three centuries ago. The days following the first industrial revolution. They hadn't got computers or robots or a controlled climate or Sleepers or anything . . . '

He broke off and thought about Sleepers. Sleepers educate you when you are asleep. The surgeon puts the Sleeper in the baby just after it is born. The Sleeper monitors and feeds the mind, intelligence, health, and behaviour of the infant-child-adolescent-adult. So the Sleeper makes a human a successful, social, civilized being. Mavis and Brian did not have Sleepers. They were merely conditioned. Brin had a Sleeper in him like everyone else: just there, inside, at the right-hand back of his skull. He touched the place.

Madi said, 'Why are you thinking about your Sleeper, Brin?' Her voice was brisk.

Brin started. 'I don't know. I suppose because they— Mavis and Brian, all those people from the time before the accident—didn't have them. So they must have been very different from us, completely different. Perhaps so

24

different that we can never really come to terms with them—'

'Never *use* them? As Reborns? Is that what you mean?'

'Well, they had *wars*, didn't they? Mavis and Brian— their scenario is set at the beginning of a *world war*! So they must be criminals. Only criminals wage war.'

'Quite so,' Madi said. 'Tell what differences you observed at first glance.'

'They're a bit heavier, and taller. A bit coarser. And . . . their heads might be smaller.'

Madi checked him. '*Coarser?*'

'Well, that could just be an impression. I mean, the clothes they wear, the things they use—they're coarse things. Things that make dirt, like the ink pens they used to write with, or the coal fire, or having to use your hands so much to do things. They even cook things themselves!'

'But you liked the soldier's toast?'

'Very much.'

'What could be coarser than that?' Madi demanded.

'I liked it very much,' Brin repeated. 'That's what I mean. Just because something is coarse, it doesn't mean it's bad. Or does it? I don't know. *You* don't know.'

'But the absence of Sleepers?' Madi said.

'Ah, that's different. That must make a great difference. But I don't know *what* difference. How can I know?'

'*Violence?*' said Madi, softly. 'Aren't you afraid of that? Aren't you afraid that, at any moment, you might have to face violence from Mavis or Brian or both?'

'*Violence?*' Brin said, staring at her. 'But that means breaking the First Law!—' He stopped short and laughed uneasily. 'I see what you mean,' he said. 'It was Sleepers that made the First Law work. Sleepers stop us from being violent. Any of us. And that's why the world has—just

25

gone on, without wars and violent crimes and murders and all that . . . '

'Sleepers were not invented until 2040,' Madi reminded him. 'And they were not used, all over the world, until 2070. So Mavis and Brian—'

'You've put me in a jungle!' Brin said. His voice shook. 'You've put me among people who could turn out to be wild beasts! People without Sleepers! Why didn't I think? Why did I let you do it? I'm not going back, I'm not—!'

Madi just laughed. 'You'll be all right, Brin. I'm right there behind the dresser, remember? As for murder and violence and all the rest of it—that was rare even in those days. Ordinary people didn't often hurt or kill each other.'

'They did! And not just one at a time! Millions at a time in the war . . . !'

She laughed. Brin began to feel foolish, then wondered how good Madi would be in dealing with violence. Probably very good. She seemed to be good at everything.

'Mrs Mossop enters the Scenario this evening,' Madi reminded him. 'You'd better change back into your 1940 clothes and get ready.'

He pulled a face and changed his clothes.

He heard Mrs Mossop in the kitchen before he saw her. She was singing. Under her singing, there was a constant dull thumping noise.

'I'll cook a rasher,' she sang,
'I'll cook a rasher,
'I'll cook a rasher for my tea.'

Then there was an unusually loud bump and Brin heard her mutter 'Damn the devil!' and make grumbling noises. He stood outside the kitchen door wondering what she would be like. He recognized the song. It was Mrs

Mossop's version of *La Cuccaracha*, a popular song of the 1940s—often played on the radio.

Now Mrs Mossop was singing 'Red sails in the sunset' in her high, vague voice. The thumping had started again. He drew a deep breath and opened the door leading in to the kitchen; on his side of the door was a sort of No-place called 'the passage'. He went into the kitchen, leaving his own century behind in this No-place.

Mrs Mossop looked up from her ironing and, with no surprise in her voice, said, 'You'll be him, then. Master Brin. Well, I never. All the way from the Bahamas. I thought they was black but you look white enough to me.'

Brin said, 'How do you do, Mrs Mossop.'

She replied, 'Well, I never,' sniffed, and went on ironing.

There seemed nothing for Brin to say or do, so he watched her. She had two flat-irons, one in her hand with a padded cloth round its handle and the other heating up in front of the range. The thumping noise was made by the iron in use as she brought it down, *thump*, on her work. Her hands were red and veined. The special electric light over the table, turned on only when Mrs Mossop ironed, lit her forearms and face. Her bare arms and face were tanned. When the iron went thump, her chin and cheeks quivered and sometimes her small gold-rimmed spectacles wobbled over her short, shining nose.

At last, Brin asked, 'Haven't you got an electric iron?'

She said, 'I don't hold with them, Master Brin,' and began to sing a song about a chapel in the moonlight. 'Oh, I love to 'ear the organ,' she sang, then went to the range to change irons. 'When we're strolling down the aisle,' she sang to herself, 'Where roses entwine.' Brin wondered what an aisle was and what he should say next, if anything.

She said, 'The Bahamas, is it? Well, I never. Where might they be when they're at home?'

27

He told her about his life in the Bahamas. It had been decided that the Bahamas were a good place for Brin to have come from: a long way from Britain, but British. Nobody would want to question too closely. Everyone would assume that his strangeness was due to coming from a strange, distant place.

Mrs Mossop hardly listened to him. She began to sing again under her breath: once or twice she said, 'Fancy that' or 'Well I never' to keep him talking. When the iron went cold she said, 'Damn the devil' and changed it for the hot one.

He tailed off and studied her face: the little mouth, pursed with effort; the heavy, worn, solid flesh; the lines round her eyes. Looking at her was like—like what? Like looking at a tree, he decided: something strong, unlikely to change, simple yet complicated. Something sure of itself. Looking at her was not like looking at a stranger. Like a tree, she was something he felt he had always known.

'Drat the cat!' she said. For Blackie the cat—Brin had only heard of it from Mavis and Brian, never before seen it—had leapt up on the pile of finished ironing, stiff-legged and straight-tailed, ready for luxury. Cats never change, thought Brin. 'Get along with you! Shoo!' Mrs Mossop said, threatening the cat with the hot flat-iron. It pushed its nose forward daintily to smell and feel the heat—pulled its head back disdainfully—then curled itself elaborately on the warm ironing, blinking its eyes at Mrs Mossop.

'That's his Lordship for you,' Mrs Mossop told Brin. 'Black Devil! Ought to be made into tennis rackets!' Brin did not know what she meant: didn't know that in the old days, rackets were strung with 'catgut'. He noticed that Mrs Mossop made a new place for her completed ironing to allow room for Blackie. 'Tea for two and two for tea,' she sang. 'None for you, and all for me.' To the cat, she said, 'Imp of Satan!' It purred.

'Staying here, then, are you?' she said to Brin a little later, making herself sociable.

'Just till my uncle comes over,' he told her.

The uncle was part of the Bahamas story. He was a Royal Air Force scientist (this might help account for Brin's brightness, and 'scientist' was a vague word anyway).

'Oh well, you'll be right enough here, I dare say, until old Hitler starts up. If he does. Then it will be back to the Bahamas for you, double quick . . . ' She wiped her brow with her arm. 'I just do the ironing and oblige,' she said. 'But *you'll* be right enough, I dare say.'

Brin knew enough by now to understand that she was talking for the sake of talking. Her words had no particular meaning. She said things that needed no answer. He wished Mrs Mossop would say real things, interesting things. He wished she would tell him all about herself and her life, her feelings and likes and dislikes. But he knew instinctively that she would not.

She cut across his thoughts by saying, 'Well, fancy, look at the clock!' He looked at it and saw nothing remarkable. 'Tea time!' she said and smiled for the first time. Her teeth were white and regular—obviously false. 'You fill the kettle, Master Brin.' To the cat she said, 'Off there, Hitler!' She piled up the ironing while he filled the kettle from the brass tap in the cold scullery, thinking, So far, she's called the cat Hitler, His Lordship, and Imp of Satan.

'I like my cup of tea,' she said to him, earnestly, rattling cups on saucers at great speed. 'But none of your dishwater. Give us that caddy . . . '

'I like soldier's toast,' Brin said, watching her put five spoonfuls in the pot. 'We don't have that in the Bahamas.'

29

'You don't want none of that,' she told him. 'You want crumpets. You look in that bag and you'll find crumpets from Osgoods. Fresh from Osgoods.'

Crumpets? He looked in her patchwork-leather bag for something that could be crumpets, but there were so many things, so many packages and bags. He pulled out a large white bag with something unpleasantly spongy and soft in it, but it couldn't be crumpets: so he went on looking. At last he had to say, 'I'm sorry but I can't find them.'

'Can't find them? You're holding them in your 'and!'

'These? These are crumpets?'

'Lord bless us and keep us—of course. Give 'em over!' She reached out her hand for the bag, impatiently. Then her face softened. 'Ah, but I dare say you've never seen a crumpet? Oh well, foreign parts, there you are, that accounts for it. Never 'ad crumpets!'

There was pity in her voice.

'Well?' said Madi. The black Senior, Tello, was there to ask questions too.

'Well, it's all going . . . well,' Brin said, uncertainly.

'What's puzzling you?' said Tello.

'Nothing, everything.' Suddenly angry, Brin said, 'It's all right, for you, you're out there just looking on and recording everything. You're wise after the event. But I'm in there, with them.'

'That's why your impressions matter more than anyone else's,' Tello said, easily. 'We need your descriptions, feelings, opinions—everything. Tell us about today.' He settled back, expectantly.

Brin's mind was a jumble. 'I understand everything about them except what they're really like,' he said.

'Well,' Madi prompted, 'are they primitives? Savages?'

'No, of course not! Obviously not! It's just that—that they're so different from us,' Brin ended lamely.

'Tell us about today,' Tello repeated. 'Tell it like a story. Start now.'

Brin did his best.

'That 'Itler,' Mrs Mossop had said, 'ought to be sliced small. 'Anging's too good for him! Put him through the mincer, that's what I'd do . . . '

'Stick him in the tripes!' Brian suggested, cheerfully.

''Ave 'is guts for garters!' Mrs Mossop said, with gloomy relish.

'Give him the Chinese water torture!' Mavis said, clasping her arms round her knees. She looked quite pretty in the glow of the kitchen range's fire. 'They fill you up with water,' she continued, 'more and more water. Through a funnel. Until you actually burst!'

'Burst?' said Brian. 'Nark it! You'd never burst!'

'They do,' Mavis said primly. 'I know they do.'

Brin had felt queasy. Savages.

'Or a machine gun,' Brian said. 'Line them up against the wall and *dang-dang-dang-dang-dang-dang*! The whole rotten lot of them! All the Nazis!'

''Ave 'is guts for garters,' Mrs Mossop repeated.

'String him from a lamp-post,' said Mavis.

'Put a tin bucket over Hitler's head and bang it till he goes barmy,' said Brian.

At this point, Brin had had enough. 'Look, can't we change the subject,' he said but Mrs Mossop interrupted. 'Look at 'Itler, then! Drat that cat, he's licking the butter off the plates!—'

'Save washing up,' Brian said. Mavis giggled.

Mrs Mossop began to sing, 'We're going to hang out our washing on the Siegfried Line.'

'And that's about all,' Brin said to Tello and Madi.

'What were you thinking?' Madi said.

31

'I was worried. A bit scared, I suppose. All that talk of violence. And yet—'

He thought of the iron thumping, and the smell of the laundry, and Brian and Mavis sighing over their homework, and Blackie the cat yawning and flexing his claws in front of the glowing kitchen range . . .

'I don't know,' Brin said. 'It gets quite cosy among the "savages" . . .'

Next evening Brin was back in the Scenario.

At nine, Brian yawned and Mavis said, 'Me too. I'm tired. I haven't finished my maths, though . . . Oh, botheration, I'll do a bit more over breakfast. You off, Brian?'

'Yep. S'pose so. Bed.'

The Scenario never changed: at nine o'clock, Brian and Mavis were programmed to become tired. Just after nine, they left the room with Mrs Mossop's words following them: 'Good night and sweet repose, half the bed and all the clothes.' She put the irons away, did noisy things to the kitchen range, sighed, laid a tablecloth over the ironing, got her coat and rusty black hat—which had to be pinned to her hair—and said, 'No rest for the wicked. Well, I suppose I must love you and leave you, Master Brin . . .'

'Goodnight, Mrs Mossop!'

'Cheeribye, Master Brin. And don't do nothing I wouldn't do.'

She would glance at Blackie suspiciously and deliver her last words. 'Don't you forget to put 'Itler out, Master Brin!'

'I won't forget, Mrs Mossop.'

'Ta-ta, then.'

'Ta-ta.'

And then Mavis and Brian were going and Mrs Mossop was gone—put back in their boxes behind the dresser, gone to limbo until the Scenario started again the next day and the players re-enacted their little play on their little stage.

There was nowhere else for them to go, of course. No bathroom and bedroom upstairs, no father and mother. The rest of the house and its people did not exist except in their minds.

Only Blackie the cat 'existed' for twenty-four hours a day. Like Brin, he lived inside and outside the Scenario.

Brin sighed and yawned and scratched his left armpit. Behind him, the big kitchen dresser swung silently on its hidden hinges and Madi was there. 'Anything to discuss?'

'No. Nothing.'

'You're bored, aren't you?'

'Yes.'

'And worried about something. Worried about what?'

'Well, they're intelligent. They're living, breathing, intelligent human beings. How much longer do you expect them to go on acting out the same old scene in the same old place, time after time?'

'As long as we want them to,' Madi replied.

'But suppose *they* don't want to? Suppose they get tired of it?'

'They're programmed,' Madi reminded him, pursing her lips. 'They have to follow the Scenario. They can't change.'

She was wrong.

'I'm sick of this,' Brian said, kicking his satchel and thumping his elbows down on the kitchen table.

'Don't *jog*! You're *jogging* me!' Mavis was doing her homework.

'Who cares?' Brian said. 'I'm sick of homework, too. And sick of you. Sick of everything.'

Mrs Mossop sang, ' "I lift up my finger and I say, Tweet, tweet, now, now, hush, hush, come, come!" '

'And I'm sick of your singing, too,' Brian told her. His face went red.

Mavis looked up from her work, shocked. 'Don't you speak to Mrs Mossop like that!' she said.

'I jolly well will!'

'You jolly well say you're sorry!'

'I jolly well won't. So there.'

Brin looked at Mrs Mossop. She held a hot flat-iron in her big red hand. What would she do with it? Brin cringed inside. Savages! The stout arm lifted, the heavy hand and iron lifted—

Thump, went the iron, on a damask serviette. Brin let out his breath and felt his heart stop pounding. The gold-spectacled weathered face showed no emotion. The iron went back and forth smoothing the serviette. She had not tried to kill Brian.

'She gets the words of the song wrong,' Brian said feebly, after a long pause. 'It isn't "Tweet, tweet, now, now, hush—" '

'What is it then, cleversticks?' said Mavis. She looked at her brother's troubled face and hissed, 'Say you're sorry.'

He muttered, 'Sorry, Mrs Mossop, I didn't mean—'

Without looking at him, she sang, ' "You always hurt the one you love, the one you shouldn't hurt at all",' then said, with an air of surprise, ' 'Ere! Where's 'Is Lordship then? Where's 'Itler been and gone? (That's all right, Master Brian.) Where's that dratted Blackie?'

Brian jumped up, anxious to please, and said, 'I'll go and see, Mrs Mossop. He ought to be here! . . . '

He went into the scullery and banged about, hiding his embarrassment by making a lot of noise looking for Blackie. Mavis started to say something to Mrs Mossop but she wouldn't listen. She said, 'Lord bless you, he meant no 'arm, drat this iron, it's colder'n yesterday's leg of mutton.'

'I can't find Blackie, Mrs Mossop!' Brian said.

'Have you looked in the WC, outside?' Mavis asked him.

'Yes. The larder, the scullery, the toilet—'

' 'E's in the garden, then, catching things,' Mrs Mossop said. 'Hope it's a rabbit, we'll 'ave stew, I don't think.' She looked up worriedly, forgetting her ironing, and began to call 'Blackie—Blackie—Blackie, come along then!' in a high, thin voice.

Brian said, 'I'll go and look for him in the garden—'

Brin panicked: there was no garden to look in, except in their minds. 'You can't do that!' he told Brian sharply.

'Oh, can't I? Who says so? Why not?' Brian demanded.

'I mean,' Brin said, 'it's dark out there. Pitch black. You can't find a black cat in a dark—'

'I'll get my torch,' Brian said. 'From the bedroom.' He stared at Brin. 'You've gone a funny colour,' he said.

'I'll get your torch,' Brin said—thinking, can Madi produce a torch for Brian?

'No, you bally well won't,' Brian said, suspiciously. 'I'll get it . . . ' He stared at Brin. 'Have you been playing with my torch?' he said at last, accusingly.

'No! Of course not. I just said I'd go and get it—'

'So you must know where it is?'

'No, I heard you *say* it was in your bedroom—'

'If you know where I left it, you must have been messing about with it! Wasting the batteries!'

'I *haven't* been wasting the batteries!'

'Oh, so you admit you've been using it?' said Brian, triumphantly.

Then Brin felt a sensation he had never felt before: something hard hit his face—something that jarred him, shook him. He saw little coloured lights and then felt what he knew to be pain, real pain. The pain came from where he had been hit.

Brian had hit him in the face with his fist.

Shocked, he shook his head and peered through the pain at Brian. People did not hit people—that was the First Law. The Sleepers did not let you hit people either. He had never been hit, but now someone had hit him. Savages! So Brian *was* a savage—

But Brian did not look like a savage, he too looked shocked, he looked just what Brin felt: embarrassed. He was backing away from Brin, his mouth trying to say words.

Mavis was hitting Brian, slapping at him and pulling at his hair and shouting, 'Pig! You're a spoiled, stupid, bad-tempered pig!'

Brian broke away from her and ran to the scullery door. He turned and shouted, 'I—I don't care! And I'm going to find Blackie!' He turned to run through the scullery, out of the back door, into the garden that did not exist.

Brin shouted, 'Please! Don't!' (In his mind, he shouted for Madi to do something, anything.) 'Brian! Come back!'

Then Brian was floundering around in the scullery—he had tripped on the step and fallen—and Mavis was crying—and Mrs Mossop was ironing, deliberately looking down at her work and going thump with the iron, not taking any notice—

A bomb began falling.

The scream of the bomb grew from nothing, getting louder and louder, a whining shriek that came nearer and nearer, so loud that it drowned the throbbing drone of the German bombers up there—

The bomb exploded, so close that the whole house shook and the glass in the big kitchen windows rattled and you could hear a house crashing and tinkling and thundering down into rubble only just down the road—

And the lights flickered, and Blackie rushed out from behind the icebox where he had been sleeping, with his eyes ablaze and his tail like a bottlebrush—

And Brian had not gone into the garden that did not exist.

Later, Madi said, 'I don't know what you are worried about. The "bomb" did what we wanted done. It stopped the situation dead.'

Brin said, 'It could have stopped everyone in the kitchen dead, *really* dead!'

'Don't be ridiculous, Brin. You don't really think for one moment that—'

'You mean, it *wasn't* a bomb?'

'Really, Brin! Of course not. Just a recording.'

'But the windows shook, the house shook—'

'It was a very *loud* recording, Brin. Loud sounds are made by moving a great deal of air. The movement of a great deal of air makes windows and houses shake.'

He said nothing and felt foolish. Eventually, he mumbled, 'A sledgehammer to crack a nut.'

'What did you say, Brin?'

'Old saying. They use it. "A sledgehammer to crack a nut" means using something much too big to achieve something small.'

'What would *you* have done, Brin, to stop Brian going into the garden?—to make him change his mind in a split second?' Madi asked.

'I don't know . . . Did you see Brian hitting me?'

'Yes. Quite a violent evening. But then, those were violent times. World War Two, remember. The Blitz . . . The bombing raids on London . . .'

'I don't see why you couldn't have done it all without violence, and bombers, and bombs.'

'Ah, but those bombs might come in useful!' she said, then flinched.

Brin saw her flinch. 'What do you mean? What do you mean? Useful for what? What do you mean, "*useful*"?'

But she had recovered. Smoothly, she said, 'Useful to make a violent interruption when something goes a little wrong within the Scenario. As it did tonight. Even more useful to find out how our Reborns stand up to danger, fear, pressure.'

'You're not telling me everything, Madi!'

'Nor will I, Brin. I will see you again tomorrow. Meanwhile, go to bed.'

'Listen, Madi!—'

'Goodnight, Brin. Do stop worrying. There's nothing to worry about.'

She smiled a perfect smile.

There was no trouble for three more evenings.

They talked of the bomb—'No. 37 down the road, completely flattened! Well, anyhow, the garage is, and all the windows.'

They talked about homework—'You are lucky, Brin, must be super not having homework to do. When is your uncle coming? No, I suppose you wouldn't know. Not with a war on.'

They had crumpets, played with Blackie.

One whole evening went by playing Monopoly. The game was so good that Brin wanted to carry on to the end and Madi 'got' his thought: that night, bedtime was after ten, an hour after Mrs Mossop had left. Mavis won and did handstands to celebrate until her face was scarlet.

It amused Brin to hear her say, next evening, 'Can't we play a game? *Do* something?' She had no memory of the game played the evening before, of course. The game had been wiped off Brian's and Mavis's memory-programme.

Brian said, 'There's a Monopoly set somewhere, let's play that.'

And Mavis replied, 'Oh, I can't stand that game, it's dull, and goes on and on . . . Let's play Ludo.'

On the fourth day, Brian said, 'I wish I was older.'

'Why?' Mavis asked.

'Well, missing the war and everything. If I were only a few years older, I'd be *in* it. Flying a Spitfire . . . '

'*You* flying a *Spit*fire! Ha ha!'

Brian was too gloomy to reply. He poked at his geography book with the nib of his fountain pen, leaving little blue-black insect marks on the cover. 'Your uncle is in the RAF, isn't he?' he asked Brin. More and more often, Brian and Mavis talked of this imaginary uncle.

'Yes,' Brin said. 'My Uncle Rick.'

'Well, when's he coming over?'

'I've told you, I don't know.'

'Does he fly?'

'Yes, but really he's a boffin. Scientific type.'

'Wish I were a boffin . . . ' Brian said. The pen spattered a little fleck of ink on Mavis's leg.

She said, 'Oh, really, must you!' Then, peevish, she said to Brian, 'I can't imagine *anything* a stupid inky schoolboy would be wanted for in this or any other war!'

'There's Civil Defence,' Brian said, still too depressed to fight back. 'The Air Raid Wardens have to have runners, don't they? Boys on bikes or something, to take messages, I could do that.'

'No, you couldn't,' Mavis said smugly. 'You're too young. They wouldn't accept you. And anyhow, both your tyres are flat, you don't take care of that bike at *all*.'

Still Brian did not fight back. 'It's just,' he said, 'that I'm sick of hanging around at home. Sick of this kitchen, and doing homework and cleaning shoes for tomorrow . . . '

'You haven't cleaned the shoes tonight so I don't see how you can be fed up,' Mavis said, enjoying herself. 'Hadn't you better clean them now, and get it over?'

'Oh, shut *up*.'

'Shut up yourself! And if,' she continued, 'you're going to act like a camel with the hump, why don't you go somewhere else to do it? You've got a room of your own, you know!'

Brin became alert. The room existed only in Brian's memory—a false memory.

Brian began to clean his and his sister's shoes. She did the putting away after the washing up and got the breakfast things ready on a tray: he cleaned the shoes. That was the arrangement. Tonight, Brian worked slowly, dully and badly.

Mrs Mossop said, 'Well, I can tell you're a good soldier, Master Brian!'

'What do you mean, good soldier?' he grumbled.

'Because you never look behind you!' she said, and smiled to herself.

'What do you mean, never look—'

Mavis was giggling. 'Don't you get it?' she said, 'Do you honestly mean you don't *get* it? You're not doing the *heels* properly, stupid! You're not looking *behind* you, see? Honestly, fancy not understanding that!'

Before Brin could even flash a thought at Madi, Brian had thrown the shoes and polish and brushes in the corner and was striding towards the kitchen door. Fortunately, he turned before Brin needed to prevent him leaving. 'If you think I'm staying here to listen to stupid little baby jokes,' he shouted, 'you've got another think coming! Because I'm not!' ('Come on, Madi, come on!' Brin prayed.) 'I'll tell you what,' Brian raged, 'I'm sick of it here! Sick of everything!'

The air-raid warning sounded just in time.

As the sirens made their banshee wail, rising and falling, Brian paused, his hand still on the doorknob. Mavis said, 'Brian, come back, don't be so silly—' but he turned the doorknob.

Mrs Mossop saved the situation. She looked at Brian through her gold-rimmed spectacles, thumped down the iron and said, 'Old Nasty's up there, and we're down here and we need a man about the house! Now then, Master Brian!'

Brian came back. Brin breathed again.

'It's not going to last,' Brin told Madi. 'It can't go on much longer. Someone's going to break out of the Scenario. Most probably Brian, but Mavis might do it too. You can't tell with her.'

'They'll do what they're told,' Madi said.

'No they won't. They're not like us. They don't *obey*, instinctively. Well, not instinctively,' he corrected himself, 'but they don't have Sleepers . . . '

'They'll obey.' Her voice was flatly certain.

'They won't. They won't, Madi.'

He left Madi and went off on his own. He was moody, dull, fed up. Had he caught his mood from Brian and Mavis? Very probably. He was sick of the Scenario, sick of the kitchen and scullery and larder and outside WC; as sick of it as they were.

Yet Mavis and Brian could not really remember it all. Each evening was a new evening to them. To Brin, it was the same dreary old play, to be enacted yet again. To them, the idea of, say, games of Monopoly or Ludo were new each time. To Brin they were a bore.

I'm more sorry for me than I am for them, he thought gloomily. And Madi and Tello—they were no help. They seemed uninterested yet completely sure of themselves. As if Brin were of no importance.

He needed exercise. He made for the Sports Centre. The brilliant lights of the Community's gleaming buildings, all metal and glass and plastic, reflected on the moving pavements: today was a rain day, Brin remembered. He stepped on the moving pavement and let it take him to the Centre, watching the play of reflected lights shift beneath his feet as the moving surfaces contrasted with the unmoving surroundings. Pretty.

But then his mind went back to Brian and Mavis. He thought about their stubbornness, quarrelsomeness, toughness. He saw in his mind the strong, unchangeable figure of Mrs Mossop, forever bent over her ironing, forever singing snatches of popular songs. 'Strangers!' he said out loud. 'Foreigners! Aliens!' And yet he liked them. He had to admit that he liked them. Did he like them more than the people of his own time, so obedient and peaceful and clever? More than himself?

He was so deep in thought that he went past the Centre. He hopped tracks, angry with himself, and got on the moving pavement going the opposite way. Sixty-five storeys high, a third of a mile wide, the Centre blazed with coloured lights. Solid pictures, holographs, tumbled and whirled. Three-dimensional acrobats hurtled past the lit windows, dancing girls beckoned, voices and music cooed or bellowed with every few metres the pavement travelled. Brin thought, That looks good: *The Venus Explosion*. Shall I see that? But he was in the wrong mood for it. The holograms showed vast explosions—molten rocks hurtled at Brin's face, one seemed to pass through his body, the noise was deafening—no, not that. Wrong mood.

The travelling pavement took him to Entrance J. J for Jimnastix. 'Yes,' Brin said to himself, and got off. Jimnastix might not have too many people or too much noise.

The uniformed girl at the reception desk smiled at him: 'What sport, Sport?'

Brin considered for a moment or two and said, 'Is the Nograv full tonight?'

She touched a switch and showed him: Only two or three people could be seen on the screen. 'You'll have it almost to yourself,' she said, still smiling brightly.

She had beautiful legs, bare and brown, smooth and slender. Brin suddenly saw Mavis's legs, in the wrinkled grey stockings: and Brian's grey and red knees, knobbly, scarred and inky over the coarse woollen school socks.

The smiling girl said, 'Nograv OK for you, then?'

'Yes. Fine.'

'Check your record?'

Automatically, he held out his left wrist to show her his ID band—the bracelet that told the State and its officials everything they needed to know about him. The information was contained in a bright dot, like the eye of a small bird, welded to the band. The ID band fitted so smoothly and snugly that you forgot you wore it. But you wore it all the time. That was the law.

'Hey!' said the girl. She was not smiling any more. She was staring at Brin. 'Check your record, I said. Well?'

'What? Oh! . . . ' Brin felt his face go red. He fumbled in the pockets of his tracksuit. Where had he put his ID band? He'd removed it when he changed for his evening in the Scenario with Mavis and Brian: changed back to his usual clothes afterwards: and forgotten to put on his ID band.

He found it. 'Here it is,' he said, shamefaced.

'Put it on your *wrist*. Show it to me on your *wrist*,' the girl said.

He did as he was told. She jerked her head at the Chek and he put his left hand flat on the Chek panel. There was the usual little click as the Chek accepted him and his ID band, but the girl said, 'That's a *Fault*, you know. Not wearing your band. You do know that's a Fault?'

'Yes. But—'

'You *do* know I'm supposed to report Faults?'

'Yes. Look, it won't happen again, it was just—'

'How many Faults make a Demerit?' she insisted.

'Three. Look, I haven't got any *other* Faults, the Chek would have told you if I'd got other Faults—'

'You kids,' the girl said. 'Just because you're kids, you think you can get away with anything.'

'So you won't report me?'

'What's the use,' she said, wearily and scornfully. 'You're a kid, you're the little darling of the Universe. No, I won't report you. But next time, you wear your ID band. You wear it *all the time*, all right?'

'All right.' He touched his heart and brain in the Sign of Politeness.

She turned her back on him even while she repeated the sign. He got his gear and walked to the Nograv, in a gloomier mood than ever.

The Nograv always made him feel better. And this evening, there were only two other people in it, both of

44

them quite old, and content to flip about quietly without shouting or showing off.

Brin thrust off from the wall and let himself float the whole sixty metres across to the other wall, fast and smooth and almost straight—just a slight curl of the spine to bring his knees up as the opposite wall rushed to meet him. *Boompf!* The soft shock of his bare feet against the soft, springy wall, then bounce back across the huge padded Nograv cell, flying so easily, so smoothly . . . because he was weightless. Free from the pull of the Earth's gravity, any gravity. Freer than a bird.

Boompf. Boompf.

He let himself bounce from wall to wall, feeling his muscles stretch with pleasure, feeling his almost naked body released from its own weights and tensions. Beneath him, the two other people had joined hands, they were going to try a Blastoff. Their hands and feet met, their arm and leg muscles tensed as they strained against each other, then—Ah!—they exploded apart, arching backwards, spinning as they flew outwards, locking their arms round their knees to speed the spin . . . *Boompf!*

The man timed it wrong, he hit the wall with his back, but the woman got it exactly right—feet against the wall, a quick straightening of the legs, and she was rocketing from the wall with the lights criss-crossing her flying body, her hair streaming out behind her. She let herself do a flab against the opposite wall to kill her speed and Brin heard her laugh at the man, who was spinning himself in a backward arc waiting for her to join him and try again. He was laughing too, apologetically.

Brin smiled and flew gently to the padded bars, springy and soft in his hands. He began to loop, faster and faster, hanging on until the speed was just right—then let go. The other bars rushed towards him. A catch-hold—now— and away again, the third bar was in his hands, his spin was reversed, still faster, and—now—his feet touched another bar but he missed the hook-on . . .

He tried again, forgetting Mavis and Brian and Mrs Mossop and Madi and Reborns; forgetting everything but his own body and the soft shock of the walls and getting the loops and hook-ons and catch-holds and reverses exactly right.

Later, the grown-ups who had been with him in the Nograv offered him a snack in the Diner. They turned out to be pleasant though a little too 'nice' and full of admiring smiles. But then, of course, as Brin knew, grown-ups felt they had to be like that with young people: important people.

Next day was another bad day. The Seniors called him before them.

The black Senior, Tello, sat beside him this time facing the big curved table. So did Madi. 'Senior Tello, you don't mind sitting with the boy?' said the Senior Elect—the one who had pretended to be peevish at the very first meeting. This time, his peevishness seemed real.

'No, we're both observers—reporters—in this matter,' Tello said, smiling to himself. 'And I'm honoured,' he continued, 'to sit beside such an important person as our young friend Brin . . . '

Brin could not tell if he was being laughed at by Tello. The faces of the Seniors told him nothing. The horse-faced Senior showed her teeth, the Chinese-looking Senior smiled about nothing in particular, the youngish female Senior with the small mouth focused her big eyes above Brin's head and the others just sat.

'Let's get on,' said the Senior Elect.

'Well, I've been with the Reborns for twenty-three

46

evenings now,' Brin began. But the Senior Elect said, 'Yes, well, we'll come to you in a minute. Senior Tello?'

Tello stood up. As he talked, he walked back and forth, his white robe swirling. His voice was not only deep and beautiful, but humorous—almost offhand. Brin found himself listening to the voice rather than the words. They hardly mattered. Tello was reporting things that Brin himself knew all about.

However, Brin did listen when Tello explained how he and Madi monitored the Scenario. 'We are behind the big cupboard called the kitchen dresser,' Tello explained. 'I am there sometimes. Madi is always there, at every session.'

'What are you doing when you are not there?' said the Senior Elect.

'I review the telerecordings and correct the Scenario, making sure that unforeseen circumstances do not develop into dangerous situations,' Tello said.

'For instance?'

'The chief danger is that the actors—the Reborns Mavis, Brian, Mrs Mossop—will try to escape the Scenario.'

'You mean, just walk out of it?'

'Yes. If one of them did that, there would be—a complication of *place*. There is nothing beyond the Scenario, the "stage setting", except a brief space of nothingness—a limbo—leading to the real world, our world. The Scenario is in a black bubble, so to speak. Our actors must never try to penetrate it.'

'What would happen if they did penetrate it?' asked the Chinese Senior.

'The experiment would then be wasted,' said Tello. 'The actors would no longer be able to believe in their roles. They would be useless to us, which would be tragic.'

'Tragic?' said the Senior Elect. 'Wasteful, perhaps.

Hardly tragic. We could always recondition the actors—give them new memory patterns.'

'I think not,' Tello said. 'We are not trying to discover what we can *make* our actors do: we are trying to discover what they *want* to do. How they *want* to behave.'

The horse-faced Senior said, 'I see what Tello means. Stress, anger, revolt, uneasiness, irritability—we must let the Reborns express these emotions as freely as possible, without conditioning. We must see them as they really are. Is that right, Tello?'

'Exactly right. We must condition them to the minimum degree necessary and stimulate them to the maximum degree. When we've pushed them to the limit, we'll know their true natures. Then we can decide how useful they can be to us later as parents and founders of new generations—'

Brin lost patience. 'You go on about anger and revolt and irritability,' he burst out, 'but that's not all Mavis and Brian show. Or Mrs Mossop. They behave less cruelly than you do! Yes, you!'

The Senior Elect said, 'Don't be impertinent.'

Brin stormed on. 'They're not just savages, idiots, cavemen, leftovers from another age! They're real people! And I don't like—I don't like the way you talk about them . . . ' he ended feebly. He sat feeling foolish. Why had he defended the Reborns? What did they matter to him?

The Senior Elect raised his eyebrows: said, 'Hm . . . ' and looked at Madi. 'Well, Madi?'

'I'll confine myself to facts,' she said, carefully. 'Brian and Mavis are larger and physically stronger than most children of our time, their heads and cranial capacities are smaller—'

'You mean, their brains are small? They are less intelligent?' asked the Chinese Senior.

48

'Their brains are smaller but their intelligences seem
. . . different. Not necessarily smaller.'

'Because they don't have Sleepers? They're merely
conditioned?'

'Because they are ruled by their *emotions*, just as we are
ruled by our Sleepers. For hundreds of years, our
civilization has been based on achieving peace—peace
between nations and peoples, peace between person and
person. But for hundreds of thousands of years, the old
people and their civilization relied on war—conflict
between nations and people, conflicts between person and
person. Even the games children played in those days were
competitive. And as you know, we have placed our
Reborns in a period of World War.'

Brin interrupted again. 'Why?' he demanded. 'Why do
that? Why couldn't they have been given peaceful, happy
lives?'

'Because peace,' the horse-faced Senior explained, 'is
too slow for our purpose. We must force the pace. The
Reborns must act out a forceful, even dangerous, play.
Things must happen *fast*.'

The Seniors went on talking. Brin did not listen. He
had other things to puzzle and worry him.

One of the things that puzzled and worried him most
was his left armpit.

Brin's left armpit itched.

It had itched for a long time. Long before the Reborns
and the Scenario.

The itch had become worse after his Nograv session.
Brin thought it must be caused by the exercise. He had
stood in front of the mirror in the changing rooms, lifted
his arm and examined his armpit. He saw little red dots,
pinpricks.

He was not surprised to see the dots. Everyone had them. But on other people, they were invisible, almost. Brin knew their cause. They were identification marks in an isotope code. If you were involved in a terrible accident that destroyed your ID band and its little bird's-eye dot, there were still the permanent codes pricked into your left armpit.

Some of the marks meant 'Extras'. On the rare occasion when a baby was born, the proud parents were told, 'There! A real baby! Your baby! Now, do you wish to apply for Extras? Any special preferences and needs?'

The parents might reply, 'Well, ours is a very musical family—'

'Then let's reinforce the baby's Musical Aptitude. Anything else?'

'I've never been very good with my hands. Always a bit clumsy.'

'Digital Dexterity, then. We'll give your baby an Extra for that.'

There would be a few routine jokes made about Fairy Godmothers—the baby would be given implants, or a modified Sleeper, or anything else needed—and the isotopic pinpricks would record the fact, just as they recorded all other essential facts about you.

That day in the Nograv, the man Brin met had said, 'I'm still not much good, but I'm getting better each session. I applied for an Extra in Physical Dexterity. A late extra, they let me take my Extra only eight months ago. Nice of them. And it's working! Mind you,' he added, 'the pinprick still itches a bit. But they warned me of that.'

Brin had never asked for or been given any late Extras. Yet his left armpit itched. And the pinpricks were raw and red, as if they were recent.

Since meeting the man in the Nograv, Brin's mind, like

his left armpit, had never stopped itching. *There was something wrong.*

Something wrong.

Mavis hobbled into the kitchen at the beginning of the next act of the Scenario play, with blood already thick and blackened on her knee and with red blood still running from the wound down the stocking of her leg.

Brin felt sick. He had never seen flowing blood—not even his own. He had never seen a wound that was not cured, instantly, by a Medipac—you slapped the pack on, the wound healed. He and his friends seldom if ever injured themselves, cut themselves, hurt each other. The discipline of the Sleepers protected them, made them avoid danger. If the Sleepers failed, there were Medipacs. If the Medipac failed, there were DomDocs—the domestic-doctor units fitted in every public and private place. If the DomDoc could not handle the situation, the injury was so serious that only the ambulance crew ever saw it.

Mavis was not really crying, she was whimpering. Her nostrils were white and she trembled. Brin started to go to her but his sick feeling turned to faintness: the blood. It was Brian who supported her, and led her to a chair; Brian who got warm water and disinfectant, and cut away the stocking, and sponged the wound.

All Brin could do was to look away from the bleeding flesh; and curse Madi and Tello and anyone else involved in drawing up such a cruel programme for Mavis. Someone, Brin realized, must actually have hit Mavis: hurt her while she slept. Now, with her wound cleaned and wrapped in a handkerchief, Mavis was really crying. The tears splashed on the floor. Brian, awkward yet determined, bent over her, his head touching hers and his red hand patting her shoulder. 'It's all right, old girl,' he kept saying. 'It's all right, old girl . . . ' Saying the strange words—'old girl'—cost Brian an effort, Brin could see. An effort of tenderness. He had never called her 'old girl' before, only 'Mave' or 'M'.

When Mavis stopped crying and let her head rest against Brian, Brin saw that Brian's eyes were filled with tears. Brian tried to pretend they were not there by shaking his head or furtively brushing his sleeve over his eyes, but at last a tear escaped and fell on the crown of Mavis's head. She must have felt its wet coldness as it trickled through her hair, for she looked up and said, 'You old sissy!' and began to laugh, shakily.

'Don't know what you mean,' Brian said, hoarsely.

'You're an old sissy!' she said, laughing and blowing her nose.

'Sissy yourself,' Brian said. 'Blubbing like that . . . How's the knee?'

'Much better, thank you very much,' said Mavis, suddenly solemnly polite, as if she were a little girl politely saying goodbye to her host at a party. 'Stupid bike,' she said. 'Stupid rotten front brake . . . '

She got up and, deliberately and carefully, put her arms round her brother's neck and kissed him. He looked stupid, almost frightened, yet kissed her cheek hastily. He mumbled, 'I'll make tea,' and went to the scullery and filled the kettle noisily.

When Mrs Mossop arrived, it was as if a party was going on. Brian and Mavis were doing ridiculous things to the sausages they were to have for supper, stabbing them with forks, dangling them in front of the cat, pretending they were the enemy—'This one's Hitler, this one's Mussolini!'—stab, stab. Brian tried to balance a sausage on his nose.

Mrs Mossop said, 'Well, I must say! Very cheerful we are tonight, aren't we!' She switched on her light and began ironing, listening and watching as Mavis acted out falling off her bicycle and cutting her knee open. She did it so well that even Brin roared with laughter; and Mrs Mossop said, 'Well, I don't know, I'm sure, Miss Mavis . . . You'd laugh if your BTM was afire!'

Madi said, 'And what did you make of them this evening?'

Brin said, 'You saw it all yourself.' He did not want to talk about it. He felt inside him a private warmth for Mavis and Brian that he did not want to share or discuss, particularly with cleanly perfect Madi. He felt she could not understand. 'An extraordinary performance!' she said, coolly.

Brin said, 'Extraordinary!' and left it at that.

Later, though, he attacked her. 'Did you have to hurt Mavis that much? Was that what the Seniors meant by ''making things less boring''?'

Madi shrugged.

'Did you see the wound?'

'Not close to,' Madi sniffed.

'Well, I did. You people think Mavis and Brian savage, crude, brutal . . . But you don't seem to mind doing savage and crude things to them—'

'You're not making much sense, and I've got to go,' Madi said. She went, leaving Brin to his thoughts.

He thought about the rest of that evening in the Scenario. When the sausages had been cooked and eaten, and Mrs Mossop had left and the party had quietened down into a sort of fireside mellowness, Brian had brought up the old subject again. 'Your uncle,' he said. 'I wish he'd actually turn up. I wish he'd come. I want to *see* him . . . '

'*I* want to see him,' Mavis said. 'I want something to happen! I want *him* to happen. When *is* he coming?'

'I don't know,' Brin said. 'It could be any time,' he said. Then, seeing their faces fall, he added, 'Soon, I suppose. Quite soon.'

'Let's have another look at his photo,' Mavis said.

Brin gave her the photo and she studied it. 'His hair's sort of brown, isn't it?'

'Yes. Darkish brown.'

'He's got a little mole sort of thing on his face. Or is it the photo?'

'No, it's like that. A sort of mole. Very small.'

'He's got nice hands. Did he always have a moustache?'

'As long as I can remember,' Brin lied.

'Is he under or over six feet tall? Does he smoke?'

'Just over six foot, I think. I'm not sure if he smokes. He used to, but not much.'

Brian took the photograph and studied it carefully. 'If he's got wings up, why doesn't he fly?'

'I told you, he's not a flying type any more. He's a boffin, a scientist.'

'But I bet he flies sometimes. As a boffin. Flying boffin.'

'Yes, I suppose so.'

'If he's a boffin, he must have had a chance to fly all sorts of planes . . . I bet he's flown more aircraft types than any ordinary pilot!'

Brin let his vanity carry him away. 'Well,' he said, pretending to make an effort, 'I know he's flown Spitfires and Hurricanes, because he started out as a fighter pilot—'

'Fighter pilot!' Brian said. 'In Hurricanes and Spits! Lucky old him!'

'And I think he did a conversion course for bombers,' Brin said. 'Wellingtons, I suppose. And Beauforts. I know he's flown Beauforts. Fighter-bombers. And some of the newer types. But of course, he doesn't tell *me* much. He can't. Official secrets.'

'Was he ever shot down?'

Brin screwed up his eyes to look wise and, proud of his knowledge of the language of the period, said, 'Not shot *down*. But he was shot *up*, over the Channel. In a Beaufort. They were strafing enemy shipping and got hit.'

'Was he wounded?' Mavis said, breathlessly.

'No. But his gunner was. And the Radio Op.' Brin combed his memory for the crew of a Beaufort. Did it carry a Radio Operator? Probably. 'The Radio Op copped it worst,' he said, shaking his head. 'But my uncle got them back to base OK. Had to land with the undercarriage up. Belly landing.'

'Gosh . . . !' Mavis said. Then, 'I do wish he'd come. I do wish we could see him, here. I do so want to meet somebody *real* . . . '

'Somebody really *doing* something,' Brian murmured. 'Somebody *real* . . . '

Brin tried to change the subject. He felt guilty and ashamed. 'Somebody *real* . . . ' The words accused him.

'If only he'd come,' Brian sighed.

'Why did you need Mrs Mossop?' Brin asked Madi and Tello. 'Why was she made a Reborn?'

'Why do you need walls in the Nograv?' Tello replied, smiling.

'To bounce off,' Brin said, sourly.

'Quite right. Mrs Mossop provides Brian and Mavis with something to bounce off. Children were used to the constant presence of adults in those days. They lived with their parents and other grown-ups. Not like today.'

'But Mrs Mossop must have taken a lot of making. And she's old. It seems a waste. You don't want old people, you want young people. People of my age—old enough to understand what you teach them, young enough to be conditioned by the teaching. Isn't that right?'

'Absolutely right. But Mrs Mossop was . . . found, and she fitted in with the period and pattern. So we reconstituted her. We made her as a companion for Mavis and Brian.'

'What do you mean, she was found?' Brin asked. 'What was found?'

'Enough to work with,' Tello said, not smiling.

'You mean, her dead body?'

'Parts of it.'

'And her clothing?'

'Parts of it.'

'A rag, a bone, and a hank of hair . . . ' Brin said.

'What was that?'

'Nothing. Just a quotation. A writer called Kipling made up those words about a woman.'

'Oh, I see.' Tello said. He yawned. 'So there you are then, Brin. The twentieth century left a rag, a bone, and a hank of hair, and we created Mrs Mossop from them.' He looked at Brin enquiringly as if asking, 'Any more questions?'

'Where did you find her?' Brin asked.

'Oh, in West London. She must have died in a bombing raid in the Hitler war. Her components were completely buried.'

'Her components?' Brin did not like the word.

'The rags and bones and hanks of hair,' Tello said, looking directly at Brin. Brin could think of nothing to say. He did not like the pictures forming in his mind. Eventually he said, 'She's a nice old lady.'

'A *useful* old lady,' Tello said, smiling again. He got up and stretched. He looked very tall and powerful, Brin thought: just as Madi, quietly sitting and making notes, looked clean, young, firm, decisive and elegant.

Not at all like Mrs Mossop.

When Mrs Mossop arrived the next evening, she seemed the same as ever and yet completely different. She seemed smaller.

Brian and Mavis noticed the change straight away. Brin did not. There was silence as Mrs Mossop got out her ironing-board, and heated the irons. It was the awkwardness of the silence that made Brin realize that something unusual had happened to Mrs Mossop.

But nothing was said. Brian and Mavis did their homework. When her iron was hot and ready, she went *thump . . . thump* just as usual. But she did not sing.

And suddenly, there was the smell of scorched linen: and Mrs Mossop was thumping the same piece of ironing again and again, not looking at it, staring straight ahead of herself, not seeing the brown scorch marks she was making.

Mavis ran to her and touched her arm and said, 'Mrs Mossop . . . ' but the old lady didn't seem to hear her. The iron went *thump* on the scorch. There was a little smoke.

Mrs Mossop started. She saw the smoke and said, 'Damn the Devil!' Then she put the iron on its heel so that it could do no more damage, threw her apron over her head, sat down in a chair and began to say, 'Damn him! Damn and blast him!' in time with her sobs. Her heavy old shoulders shook and her thin gold wedding ring glinted under the electric light against her strong, wrinkled fingers.

'It's her next door,' she said a little later. 'Mrs Hills. She's gone and the house with her. It's all gone, all gone. And her with a son in the Merchant Navy . . . '

Mavis and Brian said nothing, Brin noticed. They moved about slowly, not looking at the old lady, not answering anything she said. They got cups and saucers, filled the kettle, warmed the pot and made tea. All this time, Mrs Mossop talked, dabbing at her eyes behind her glinting gold round spectacles, telling them of the raid last night: of the land mine, and the houses flattened, and the fire engines and ambulances and the vicar and the Civil Defence and Mrs Hills being dragged out—'but it was no use, you could see at a glance, she was gone. We was neighbours twenty-three years, that's a long time . . . '

They gave her tea. She drank a little of it and said, 'I *do* like a cup of tea . . . '

They talked to her, soothingly. She answered normally. Once she broke into a swearing tirade about Hitler, using words that even Brin knew to be forbidden. But then she said, 'Oh, dear, oh dear, beg pardon, you mustn't mind me. I'm not myself and that's a fact . . . '

Brin thought, No, you're not. You're an old woman now, an old, old woman.

Using the ugliest of the words he had learned from Mrs Mossop, he cursed Madi, Tello, the Seniors, and the Reborn programme. They had made Mrs Mossop weak and old and tearful just as an 'experiment'. It was cruel. It was wrong.

Mrs Mossop left early, and there was silence when she was gone. Brin broke the silence by saying, 'It's rotten! Poor Mrs Mossop! What's she done to deserve—'

Brian said, 'No good talking about it. Change the subject.'

Brin turned to Mavis, shocked by Brian's apparent coldness: but she too said, 'Talk about something else.'

'*What* else?' Brin demanded.

'I don't know. Anything. Oh, I know—tell us more about your Uncle Rick!'

Brin tried to get out of it, but couldn't. And for the next hour, he made up stories about his uncle, stories so exciting that Mavis's eyes sparkled and Brian said, 'Gosh! Go on! What happened next?'

Brin told him, piling thrill upon thrill. After all, it was better than thinking about Mrs Mossop . . .

To the Elders, however, Brin spoke what was in his mind when he next appeared before them.

By now he felt he had got to know them. Tello, the one he saw often, was almost his friend. The horse-faced Senior turned out to be a surprisingly warm, pleasant woman at heart. The Chinese-looking Senior was a discreet, private person whose smile, Brin now knew, meant very little—it was as if she put her smile on in the morning with her clothes and wore it all day. But she was always pleasant to Brin. She listened carefully when he spoke, then smiled and nodded agreement.

The other Seniors, too, were now familiar figures in Brin's mind. Not friends; neutrals. Standing (or more likely sitting) before the white-gowned figures of the Seniors had never frightened Brin; he was too conscious of the superiority of his youth to feel fear. He felt only tension: a tightening of his mental muscles. He was always aware that he must show himself at his best—keep his mind alert and fast-moving, his words clear and vivid, his face and manner decisive.

Today, he felt nothing of this familiar tension. He felt only a deep and determined anger that he intended to express. He would talk. They would listen.

The Seniors made the Sign of Politeness. Brin barely bothered to sketch his reply. Before his hands had stopped moving, he was speaking. 'About Mrs Mossop,' he said. His voice was cold and clear. 'What you did to her was savage, stupid, and brutal.' He folded his arms across his chest and sat back in his chair, watching the faces of the Seniors.

Their reactions were not at all what he expected.

The Chinese-looking Senior smiled and nodded. The horse-faced Senior put her head very slightly to one side and looked back levelly into Brin's eyes with an expression of friendly interest. The Senior Elect, the peevish one, did not bother to become peevish: he continued to write with his old-fashioned pen on a tablet of paper, without even looking up. Tello seemed gloomy and preoccupied. He took no notice at all of Brin. Brin was surprised and hurt. Surely Tello was his friend?

Only Madi seemed aware of the importance of what Brin had said—of the rude violence of his words and the sincerity behind them. She had been standing beside him. Now he felt her hip against his shoulder and heard a whispered, warning murmur, 'Brin! You shouldn't—'

The Senior Elect looked up at last, and said, 'What? What was that, Brin? I don't think I heard . . . ' And now his faded yet piercing eyes were locked on Brin's, expecting and demanding that the words be repeated.

Brin steeled himself and said again. 'What you did to Mrs Mossop was savage, stupid, and brutal.'

This time, the words seemed to echo in the big room, to bounce uselessly against the old, experienced faces of the Seniors.

'Savage,' said the Senior Elect, tonelessly. 'Ah, yes. Savage . . . stupid . . . brutal.' He wrote the words down. The Chinese-looking Senior smiled. Tello brooded. The horse-faced Senior began rubbing her long nose with a long finger. To Brin, the silence was like a long, cold corridor.

At last the Senior Elect spoke. The old eyes drilled into Brin's. 'Is that all you want to say?'

Brin did not want to reply. He did not trust his voice to stay steady. He gulped and opened his mouth—

The Senior Elect held up a thin hand to prevent him speaking. 'You don't say "unnecessary",' he said, mildly. '"Unnecessary" isn't one of your words. So I suppose you understand that our treatment of Mrs Mossop was *necessary*. Now, had you said the word "unnecessary", Brin, I would have been obliged to reply by saying to you—' he broke off and turned to the other Seniors, 'What would I have said to him, do you think?'

The Chinese-looking Senior smiled brightly at Brin and in her high, clipped voice suggested, '"Don't be a silly boy!" Something like that, perhaps?' The Senior Elect nodded approvingly.

'"Don't be an impertinent child,"' suggested the horse-faced Senior, in a pleasantly experimental tone of voice.

'"Shut your stupid mouth!"' said another Senior, helpfully.

Brin's mouth opened and closed soundlessly. The big room seemed to spin whitely around him. They were being rude! Deliberately rude! To him! To Brin! And Tello said nothing. He did not even look up.

'No,' said the Senior Elect, 'None of you conveys quite my meaning. Now let me see, let me see . . . Ah, I have it. A long time ago, Brin, there was a little poem that fond parents spoke to their children. I will recite that poem to you and you will memorize it. This is the poem:

> Speak when you're spoken to
> Do as you're bid,
> Close the door after you,
> There's a good kid.

Have you memorized it, Brin?'

The eyes of the Seniors regarded him with mild interest as Brin struggled to reply. 'Yes . . . ' he said, at last.

'Then let us hear it!' said the Senior Elect. 'Recite it for us, Brin!'

'*Speak when you're spoken to . . .* ' Brin said, chokingly.

'It would be better if you stood up,' said the Senior Elect. 'Stand up, Brin, and continue.'

'*Do as you're bid*,' Brin said. His knees trembled and a black bile of shame and anger gagged him. '*Close the door after you*,' he continued.

The Senior Elect finished the poem for him. '*There's a good kid*,' he said, soothingly and poisonously. 'Take him out, Madi. And let him wait somewhere out of people's way until Tello is ready to give him his next instructions.' He gave the Sign of Politeness. Brin, hands shaking, responded and let Madi lead him from the room.

At the door, the mild voice of the Senior Elect called, 'And close the door after you, Brin, remember? There's a good kid!'

Madi had to lead Brin away from the great room. He could not see for tears of shame and fury. The pity in her voice when she said, 'Wait there, Brin,' made his pain all the worse.

When she was gone, he rubbed his eyes savagely, gritted his teeth, and strode to the door of the clean, mean, bleak little waiting room to which Madi had taken him. He twisted the handle of the door. A square panel above the door lit up and showed the word NO; a recorded voice said, 'You are not free to leave. Please take a seat. You are not free to leave.'

He twisted the handle again, using all his strength. Something gave. The door opened.

'You are not free to leave,' the voice bleated. But he left

the room and the voice and the building behind him, and walked blindly on, faster and faster, into the city.

You were allowed to walk in the city. Few people did: the moving pavements, the walkways, walked for you. But you could walk if you wished and did not mind the curious stares and the possibility of being stopped by the police and asked to identify and explain yourself.

So Brin walked, barely knowing he was walking. He walked without seeing the great silver towers, the wide green parks with each tree named and labelled, each bird and animal identified on the TV displays. Automatically, he wove his way through the pedalecs—the silent electric bicycles that glittered like insect-swarms in certain streets and special areas.

Above him, the clean, glassy building soared fifty storeys high, seeming almost to touch the great transparent curve of the Ecodome that packaged the city and made its atmosphere. Around him, the cars mewed and whined, slowly bumbling along the roads, blindly following the get-you-there tracks under the road surface. Sometimes a line of cars was stopped, each car nudging squishily at the one in front; only then did the 'drivers' and passengers look up from their in-car TV screens. Sometimes a 'driver' would crossly prod the tabs and buttons in front of him to make the car go forward again. Of course, it made no difference.

Under Brin's feet, the city pumped and whirred and hummed and growled and vibrated. Below ground, the real business of the city went on—the drains and trains, power plants and factories, nature reserves and laboratories, computer complexes and service depots, protein banks and weathermaker plants . . .

Brin paused, by habit, at one of the city's eight Great

63

Parks. This was the second biggest—almost an acre. Trees, shrubs, waterfowl on the little lake and people, people, people . . .

A big coloured moth flew almost into Brin's face, startling him. Immediately the nearest TV screen showed a still picture of the moth and named it, in English and Latin.

'As if I cared,' Brin said.

He became aware of the itching of his left armpit. It itched abominably. Why? Obviously because he was hot— hot with rage and resentment, burning with fury. He scratched his armpit furtively, hoping no one would see; then, from habit, made the Sign of Politeness to the world in general.

Hot with anger, raging hot . . . and also cold. Cold with an iceblock of fear in the very centre of him. The fear made a kind of core in his body. He had got everything wrong, misunderstood everything. Particularly the Seniors. He had misunderstood their conscious power, their arrogance, their cold authority, their chilly certainty, their cruelty.

He had failed to understand the Seniors. Had he failed also to understand himself? Obviously. He had thought of himself as a little king, a power in the land, someone automatically entitled to respect and smiling agreement. He was nothing of the sort.

He had thought that when he pointed out to the Seniors the error of their ways—their cold cruelty to a poor, simple old woman—they would be uneasy and ashamed and anxious to oblige Brin by putting things to rights. Nothing of the sort.

The Seniors had treated him just as they had treated Mrs Mossop: with a chilling, humiliating show of power. 'Don't be a silly boy.' 'Speak when you're spoken to, do as you're bid.' That was how they thought of him.

'I'll show you,' Brin snarled. But show them what?

What had he got to show them? He was just a small cog in this big, glittering wheel of a civilization. And his armpit itched.

It itched so furiously that he gave his mind to it. He sat down, folded his arms and secretly, privately, gave himself the pleasure of a good long scratch. There! Just there! Better! Was anyone watching him? No, once more, just there! Much better. But when he stopped, the itching started again.

He jumped out of his skin when the voice behind him said, 'Who are you?' and a huge, inhuman figure towered over him, looking at him through masked beetle eyes. A uniform of Adamant: the nozzle of the suit's Viper pointing at him. Policeman. Special Force.

'Check your record,' said the policeman, giving the Sign of Politeness. Returning the sign, Brin felt better. The policeman's inhuman voice said a few words; but the words were spoken with the old, familiar, welcome tone of friendly respect: the respect that all people of Brin's age were entitled to.

Without bothering to stand up, Brin showed the policeman his ID band. An agreeable grunt came from the mouthpiece of the Adamant suit—'Mmmm. Fine. Everything all right?'

'Fine,' said Brin. 'Just fine.'

'Just routine check,' said the policeman. 'Just making sure you're all right.'

'I'm all right. Fine. Thank you.'

'Have a good day, then. Rain tomorrow, remember! Enjoy the sun today, right?'

'Right.'

The policeman gave the Sign of Politeness. Brin returned it. The policeman went away, walking like a broad machine, the man's muscles multiplied by those built into the Adamant suit. Brin watched him go, the sun glinting on the silver-white fabric and the white dome of helmet. Polite policeman. Quite right to be polite. 'After all,' Brin murmured, 'I am Brin . . . '

But who was Brin? Why did Brin have an itching armpit? How can an armpit itch from tiny pinpricks made years and years ago, in babyhood? Should he apply a Medipak, or go to a DomDoc? The itching could be stopped, easily, immediately, Brin knew that.

But he knew too that stopping the itching would not answer the questions. Why were the Seniors cruel? Why did his armpit itch? Why, why, why? Brin walked on. A second policeman stopped him.

This policeman was invisible inside a Trubble-Bubble, a patrol car. The Trubble-Bubble silently glided alongside Brin and its voice said, 'Hi. You're Brin, aren't you? Got a minute?'

'Certainly,' Brin said and gave the Sign. The Trubble-Bubble flashed its answering Sign and its voice said, 'Like to step inside?'

'No. I'm busy.'

'Fine. Fine. Whatever you say. But your friends are worried about you.'

'What friends?'

'A particular friend. Tello. Senior Tello. Very anxious to get in touch with you. Wants to see you particularly.'

'Sorry, I'm busy.'

'Fine. Whatever you say. Sure you won't step inside?'

'I told you, I'm busy.'

'Fine. Well, that's it, then.'

The Sign of Politeness flashed again and Brin was making his reply—

The Trubble-Bubble swelled, its smooth teardrop shape expanded outwards towards Brin, and suddenly its soft, jelly-glassy pick-ups were round Brin's body, locking his arms, making it impossible to move—and then part of the

Trubble-Bubble's skin turned inside out and Brin and the pick-ups were in the Trubble-Bubble, not outside it—

Brin tried to struggle, but the pick-ups, so soft and smooth and gentle, smothered him, held him in their firm jelly. He shouted but his yells of rage were smothered by the Trubble-Bubble and the Trubble-Bubble's voice kept saying, 'Fine, fine, just fine, take it easy now, everything's fine.'

And now the Trubble-Bubble was accelerating away, smoothly, silently, comfortably, adjusting its shape and size to its new passenger, gently forcing Brin to sit. Brin shouted: 'Let me out!' The policeman's voice said, 'Shut your wet mouth,' and his elbow slammed into Brin's ribs.

The pain was shocking, but not as shocking as the realization of what was being done to him. For the second time in one day, Brin was being humiliated—beaten down—taught his place. And not as shocking as the thing that was happening to his body: it was heaving and shaking, making noises. He was crying, actually crying.

In a hidden underground part of the Centre, the Trubble-Bubble ejected Brin right at Tello's feet. 'Hallo, hallo, hallo!' Tello said, smiling hugely. '*What* a day you're having, Brin!'

Brin had to let Tello help him to the lift.

'You can't do this!' Brin shouted, 'How dare you!'

'Speak when you're spoken to, remember?' Tello said, smiling. But Brin could sense the man's anger. The walls of the hot little room seemed to totter and sway round Brin, pressing in on him. It was all unbelievable. Respect! There was no respect! The world had gone mad and now the madness was smiling at him, almost laughing at him, with perfect white teeth.

'Open that door,' he told Tello. 'I'm leaving!'

'Do as you're bid,' Tello grinned.

Madi came in, brisk and clean and long-legged. Brin turned to her. 'Help me!' he demanded. 'Make Tello let me go! Stop him being rude!'

She stared at him without expression, then said—to Tello, not to Brin—'He just won't *learn*, will he? With his IQ, you'd think he'd be able to *learn*.'

'Learn what?' Tello prompted, laughing softly.

'Learn to do what he's told. Learn how unimportant he is. Learn that he's just a stupid kid who's got to obey his elders.'

'He'll learn,' Tello said, still laughing. Then he did something Brin found unbelievable: something his whole education told him to be almost impossible. His big hand darted out and seized Brin's chin—the whole lower half of his face—in an iron and velvet grip. Brin could feel his lips twist into a ridiculous shape, like a gaping fish mouth, and heard the absurd protesting noise the hand forced out of him.

'Listen and learn, Brin,' Tello said, wagging Brin's head with his big hand. 'Listen and learn, right?'

Brin made a strangled sound. The big hand hurt. So did the suspicion that Tello was enjoying himself— enjoying giving pain.

'You're merely part of an experiment, Brin. Just a little part of a big experiment. The experiment will go on and on until it succeeds. It will go on with or without *you*, Brin.'

Tello let Brin free, then settled back easily in his chair.

'*You* don't matter, the *experiment* matters, do you understand? *Brin* doesn't matter, but the *Reborns* matter. We can always get another Brin but we can't easily replace Brian and Mavis and Mrs Mossop. Clear so far?'

Brin mumbled. Madi said, sharply, 'Answer Senior Tello properly!' and Brin said, 'Clear . . .'

Tello said, 'The Seniors aren't pleased with me. The experiment isn't going well enough or fast enough, Brin—'

'That's not *my* fault!' Brin burst out.

'There you go again,' Tello said, 'thinking of yourself! *You* don't matter!—unless you *interfere* with the experiment—'

'By interrupting it,' Madi said. 'By feeling sympathy. Or by taking sides with the Reborns against what you call "injustice" or "unkindness".'

Tello held up a hand to silence her. 'Or, Brin, by doing anything at all except what we tell you to do. We don't want your opinions about our policies and actions. We want only your obedience. Clear?'

Madi flicked Brin's shoulder—another unbelievable rudeness—with the back of her hand. 'Answer Senior Tello!' she said.

'I understand,' Brin muttered.

'He understands,' Tello said to Madi, grinning at her. 'And he's going to be a good boy from now on, isn't that right, Brin?'

'Particularly this evening,' Madi said. 'He's going to be a very good boy this evening.'

'So he is, so he is,' Tello said. 'Because this evening is important. This evening, we intend to try a new twist. A bit more pressure—'

'Pressure?' Brin said, suddenly afraid. He saw in his mind's eye the faces of the Reborns—Mavis making soldier's toast and Mrs Mossop banging down the iron and Brian polishing the shoes; and the time when Mavis cut her knee; he saw the inefficiency and grubbiness of their world, and its sudden glowing warmth and hidden strength—a warmth and strength that had no place in his world.

'A bit more pressure,' Tello said. 'Quite a bit more.' Was he enjoying himself, Brin wondered; or was he forcing himself to 'act tough', to impose himself? Tello stood up and stretched. Madi bit her lower lip.

Brin said, 'What do you mean? What's going to happen this evening?'

Tello stopped stretching and said, 'Mrs Mossop.'

'What about her? What are you doing to her?'

'Writing her out of the Scenario. We don't need her any more.'

Brin felt his mouth go dry.

'We're killing her off,' Madi said, resting her slim brown hand on her knee.

'What do you mean? You can't mean—'

'Killing her off. She gets an electric shock from that switch she uses to turn on her ironing light. The shock kills her. We've boosted the current.' Madi's fingers stroked her rounded knee.

'But why? *Why*?'

'Don't need her. I told you. We want to see how the children react to her loss: to coping by themselves.'

'But I can't see *why*—' Brin's voice failed him.

Madi, suddenly furious, jumped to her feet. 'Oh, for heaven's *sake*!' she shouted. 'He's so dim!'

Tello waved her aside. 'Brin, I've told you before and I'll tell you again. But for the last time. *Sleepers*, Brin. Our civilization runs on Sleepers. We don't fight because we don't want to because of Sleepers. We don't commit crimes because we don't want to because of Sleepers. We've got communities, societies, nations—a whole world—that lives in peace and prosperity because of Sleepers.'

'I know all that,' Brin said. 'But why can't you simply make Reborns and give them Sleepers? Why must you torture them, hurt them—'

Madi, her voice still filled with a disgusted boredom, said, 'Our generation is about the fifth Sleeper generation.

70

The early generations resisted Sleepers. There were outlaws, renegades, rebels—people who *resisted* Sleepers—until quite recently. Who told you Sleepers are infallible? Who knows how well Sleepers will work on early generations of Reborns?'

Brin thought, I suppose she's right. I don't know . . . His mind whirled. His armpit itched.

Tello's voice stopped him thinking further. The Senior said, 'Sleepers aren't a cure-all—an instant remedy. It's taken generations to develop—with the aid of Sleepers— the people of our world. Even today, we get our failures and throwbacks . . . People who revolt, who use violence, who defy society. We don't talk about them. We hide them away. We call them Dissidents. It's a nice soft word . . . '

'Your precious Reborns,' Madi said, 'could be incurable Dissidents.'

'But you haven't even tried Sleepers on them!' Brin said.

Madi said, 'We condition them. Not too much but enough. We let them remember some things—let them have thoughts to build on—thoughts about you and that Uncle Rick character. We condition them for safety: to keep them in the Scenario. It could take years—lifetimes—generations to know if complete Sleepering is possible.'

'And now,' Tello said, 'all we can do is to measure their difference from us by testing them to the limit. Putting them to the sort of test that invites a dramatic, even violent, response.'

'They take a violent test this evening,' Madi said.

'You help,' said Tello. 'You don't hinder. You help. Understand?'

Brin muttered, 'I help.' For the second time that day, he felt tears in his eyes.

The evening started in the same old way. Brian throwing

his satchel in the corner, Mavis making him pick it up. Ludo on the battered old board, bickering about who should make the tea. 'I made it last time!' 'You didn't!' 'I did!' 'Well, I'll do it when I've won this game.' 'Fat chance! Come on six, I want another six . . .'

Mavis got a six, chortled, and put out her last man. She already had two home. Brian scowled, threw a two, and groaned. One of Brin's men was right behind him, only three squares away. 'Three! Three!' Brin prayed, rolling his eyes up to the grimy ceiling, criss-crossed with the dusty ropes and slats and pulleys of the airing rack. 'Three! *Please*!' Brin cried. For the moment, the game had carried him away. He had forgotten Mrs Mossop. He threw the dice, got a four and beat the floor with his fists while Brian shouted, 'Ha-ha! Ha-ha! One step behind you! Just you wait!'

Then Mrs Mossop came in. 'Well, that's one way to win the war, I suppose,' she said. '*Ludo*, at *your* age!' She sniffed, and dumped her carrying bag on the ironing-table. 'They caught it down by the fire station last night, what a mess, the bank's got all its windows broke,' she said. 'Pity Jerry didn't blow the safe open, I'd have bought a ticket for that . . . And no tea, you haven't even put the pot to warm, well I *must* say!'

She began her high, weak singing—'Look at the *coff*in, bloomin' great *hand*les, ain't it *grand* to be bloomin' well *dead*!'—and Brin tried not to see the old gypsy-like face or to hear her singing, cosy as a tea-kettle. He did not even notice when Brian threw a one—yelled 'Whoopee!'—and swept his man off the Ludo board. He felt the white chill of despair invade him.

Mavis noticed. 'You all right?' she said. 'You look all funny . . .'

'He's broken-hearted!' Brian said. 'I've sent him home again!' And he slammed Brin's man back into its starting-place. 'Now I'm going to get you, Mave!' he chuckled.

'*Are* you all right?' Mavis said to Brin.

'I was just . . . just thinking.'

'Thinking about what?' Mavis insisted.

'Oh, come on, let's play if we're going to play!' Brian said, shaking the dice.

'Just thinking. Thinking about nothing, really,' Brin said. He glanced sideways at Mrs Mossop. She was not yet ready to start ironing: she was getting cups and saucers out and peering into the tin tea-caddy with the pictures of Queen Mary and King George V on its sides.

'Were you thinking about *him*?' Mavis said, leaning forward. 'About your Uncle Rick?'

'No. Yes. I was thinking about Uncle Rick,' Brin lied. 'Wishing he'd turn up.'

'It's your *go*!' Brian said, crossly. But Mavis was hardly listening. Automatically, she threw the dice—a six; threw again—a four; and put her last man home. 'What a rotten swizz!' Brian shouted, furious. 'First a six, and then that four! Honestly!'

Mrs Mossop poured the water into the brown teapot. She would not go near the deadly light over the ironing-table for quite a time yet.

'Uncle Rick's got to come to England some time, hasn't he?' Mavis said, her face close to Brin's. 'They have conversion courses, don't they—you know, to learn to fly new aircraft types and things like that? So he's got to come here some time, hasn't he?'

Mrs Mossop poured the tea, singing, 'Sally, Sally, born in our alley.'

Brin said, 'Oh yes, he's coming over. He must. You saw his letter, he said he was coming over but didn't know when.'

Brian complained, 'I just don't know where she gets

her luck, I mean, all those sixes! It's against the law of averages!'

Mrs Mossop put two flat-irons on the hob of the kitchen range.

They drank their tea. 'He'll get leave, of course,' Mavis said.

'He probably won't,' Brian said spitefully, still angry about Mavis's luck with the dice. 'He might not get leave at all. Don't you know there's a war on?'

Mrs Mossop went to the irons, picked one up and held it close to her cheek to test the heat. 'The Spaniard that blighted my life,' she sang, and put the iron back in front of the coals. Not hot enough.

Mavis, squatting on the floor in front of the kitchen range, had her chin in her hands. She stared into the fire then into Brin's eyes. 'If only!' she said. 'If only he'd come! I think about him all the time. I wish and wish and wish! I . . . *concentrate* on making him come—on hearing his footsteps in the passage outside, then his hand knocking on the door, and his voice calling out!' Her fists were clenched, her eyes wide.

Brian said, 'That's funny—' and Brin thought he was going to make a jeering remark. But he didn't. Instead, he said, 'I do the same thing. I concentrate on him coming . . . You know, imagining his face—I mean, we've seen the photographs . . . and wishing he'd appear.'

He paused and said, 'It's all so dull! The war and the blackout and everything. I thought it would be exciting, the war, but it's not, we seem to spend our whole lives in this mouldy old kitchen. I wish he'd come! Why doesn't he come?'

Mrs Mossop sang, 'One day my prince will come,' but Mavis and Brian ignored her. Brin stared at them, anxious and guilty. He had created the dream. Now it was taking hold.

Mrs Mossop said, 'Them irons ought to be ready by now.' She reached out to switch on the light over the ironing. Brin reacted only just in time.

'Wait!' he shouted, his voice almost a scream.

Brian, jerked out of his dream, said, 'What? Wait for what?'

Mavis said, 'What's happening? What are you shouting for?'

Brin, searching for a lie, muttered, 'Sorry. I thought I heard something. Something outside.'

'*Uncle Rick?*' Mavis breathed.

'*Uncle Rick?*' Brian said, his eyes fixed on the door.

'Uncle Rick,' Mrs Mossop said, shaking her head. 'You and that uncle of yours . . . ' Again she reached out her hand to the switch that was to kill her.

Before Brin could act—before another word could be spoken—there was an echoing thump of footsteps—a double rat-tat on the kitchen door—and a young man's voice called, 'Heh! Blast, it's pitch-dark out here—heh, anyone at home?'

Mavis flew to the door and opened it.

Framed in the doorway, tall and smiling, was Uncle Rick.

It was impossible that it was true, but it was true. He stood there: Uncle Rick. He was real. His big bushy moustache, as wide as the young, jolly face, was real. The worn blue RAF uniform, with its medal ribbons on the tunic, was real. The spotted scarf, the brown eyes, the battered holdall—they were all real.

And all, Brin knew, impossible.

'Hello, kids!' said Uncle Rick. 'Let's go out and paint the town red!'

Mavis ran to him and flung her arms round his waist, almost crying with pleasure.

Brian said, *'You're him!'* and stared. Then, remembering his manners, silently held out his hand, unable to speak.

Brin hung back, not knowing what to think or say: the only word in his mind was, 'Impossible!'

'Shake hands with your uncle, Brin!' Rick called. And Brin, uncertainly, took the man's hand. It was a real, solid, flesh-and-blood hand. It gripped Brin's hand strongly.

'You're Mrs Mossop!' cried Uncle Rick, and strode across the floor to shake her hand. She changed, before their eyes, into a flirtatious young woman, dimpling and flirting with her eyes. 'Oo!' she said, 'A pleasure, I'm sure!' and dabbed at the hair over her ears.

'Well, where are we off to?' said Uncle Rick.

'Out!' Mavis said. 'Anywhere, but *out*! Out of here! Take us out, Uncle Rick!'

'No!—' Brin said, but nobody listened to him, nobody heard.

'Bang on!' said Uncle Rick. 'Quick, then! We're off!'

'I must change—' Mavis began, but Uncle Rick caught her up, whirled her round on his arm, and said, 'No time! You look smashing! Tally ho!'

Mavis and Brian ran round in circles, changing shoes, running combs through hair, pulling collars straight, gabbling with delight. Brin, his mouth dry, tried to imitate their enthusiasm while his mind raced. Mrs Mossop nodded and beamed, beamed and nodded. 'You're never going out like that, young lady!' she told Mavis. 'Your hair's like a spider's lounge . . . ' She dabbed at Mavis with a comb, while Mavis hopped up and down and cried, 'Oh come on! Do hurry! Let's go! Let's get *out*!'

And then Brin found himself actually at the door of the kitchen, trying to think of something—anything—to put off the fatal moment when the door opened to limbo, nothingness; and the Scenario was torn apart; and Madi and Tello stepped in with—with what? With destruction, fire, an explosion, nerve gas? 'Just a minute!' he said, feebly. 'What about Mrs Mossop?'

'Coming too!' smiled Uncle Rick.

'But we can't leave the house—'

'Can't take it with us, either!' Uncle Rick said, laughing.

'The blackout—' Brin said, hopelessly.

'Come *on*,' Brian said. 'Paint the town red! Let's go!'

'Tally ho!' shouted Uncle Rick. 'Formate on me! Look out, London, we're on our way!'

He turned the worn brass handle of the kitchen door and led the way out.

They stepped from the kitchen into black nothingness. Their footsteps and cheerful cries raised no echoes.

Holding hands, they stumbled on—'Crikey, it's so dark!'—'Who was worrying about the blackout, Brin?'—'Ooo! It's spooky!'—and giggled and blundered and tripped their way towards a faint light ahead of them.

'Front door, where are you?' called Uncle Rick. Then—'Funny sort of door, doesn't seem to want to open!—No, wait—ah! Got you!' Suddenly the five of them were in blazing light, lights everywhere, light that shifted and winked and glared, blinding light.

They were in a street of the city that only Brin knew and understood.

'But it's not possible!—' Mavis gasped, staring at the whirling lights, the glare, the glassy towers.

'I don't understand!' Brian muttered, eyes wide.

'What price the blackout . . .?' Uncle Rick muttered.

'That pavement's moving, it's going along all by itself!'

said Mrs Mossop. Her mouth was a surprised O. More than any of them, she looked out of place in the city of the future: the coloured lights of the city painted her worn old face and clothes a hundred shifting colours, none of them right.

Brin kept quiet and worried. There was nothing he could say or do. He could only wait for *them*—Madi, Tello, and the other Seniors—to take action: to do something to remove Mavis, Brian, Mrs Mossop, and Uncle Rick. They were in the wrong time, the wrong place. They *looked* wrong (but so far, not one of the busy people passing by had looked their way! It was rude to stare, thank goodness). But surely one of Brin's party would soon start asking unanswerable questions about the clothes worn by the people of the city, the lights, the structures, the words and pictures on the signs?

It was Uncle Rick who supplied an answer to the impossible. To Brin's astonishment, Uncle Rick began to chuckle. 'Well, *well*! This beats everything! I've *heard* of places like this, but never thought I'd live to see one!'

'Places like what?' Brin said.

'Dummy targets!' said Uncle Rick, still chuckling. 'Big spoofs! But on this scale!—'

'What do you mean?' Mavis said, skipping along beside him, her arm through his, her face radiant.

'Keep moving!' Uncle Rick said. 'Keep walking! I want to see this—and I don't want to be picked up by the MPs!'

Now they were following Uncle Rick, walking briskly among the people of the city. Still nobody looked at them. The very drabness of their clothes provided some sort of concealment. 'MPs?' Brian said. 'I don't understand—'

'Military Police!' Uncle Rick told him. 'Keep walking! Don't look so surprised, try and look normal! Don't you see, we're not supposed to be here—not supposed to know such a place exists! We could be picked up at any moment! But I must see it all!'

'Dummy target, you said dummy target!' Brian insisted. 'What did you mean?'

Uncle Rick's voice was excited but low as he explained. 'Dummy targets! To fool old Jerry, don't you see?' he said. 'Old Jerry comes over with his bombers to hit London or another big city—can't find it always, because of the blackout—gets confused, doesn't know where he is—then suddenly sees all these *lights*! So what does old Jerry think?'

'I don't know, I don't understand—' Mavis said.

'He thinks he's over a *neutral country*!' Uncle Rick hissed, unable to stop himself grinning at the cleverness of it all. 'Thinks he's over Sweden or Switzerland— anywhere. Anywhere but England! All these lights, just like peacetime—poor old Jerry thinks a gremlin's got at his navigational aids, or the navigator of the plane has gone barmy, and the whole operation's gone for a burton!—so he radios back to base, and we intercept the radio calls, and our fighters are waiting!—' He began laughing out loud, then stopped.

'Up there!' he said, quietly. 'No, don't stop walking, and don't stare—but look up there! On top of that building!' They looked and saw strange aerials, delicate grids, spouting from a skyscraper. Brin knew what they were: climate-control sensors, part of the system that controlled the climate of the sealed city. But Uncle Rick said, '*Radar!* Or some sort of radio-beam distorter, to mess up all the Jerry signals, I suppose that's it—make their navigational equipment give duff gen, make them think they're hundreds of miles off-target!' He whistled admiringly and said, 'But a whole city! A thing on this scale! All these people working on it, living in it! And we used to think the Jerry scientists hot stuff!'

Brin listened, half-stupid with anxiety and fear, to Uncle Rick's words. The Seniors would do something, soon. What? His left armpit itched savagely. Why? His mind flickered and changed like the lights of the city.

Above the heads of the crowd, he could just pick out the smooth, domed top of a Trubble-Bubble. 'Uncle Rick!' he said, warningly, but Uncle Rick would not listen to him: he was talking of decoy raids, mock attacks and all the tricks opposing air forces played on each other. Brian and Mavis hung on his words. Mrs Mossop hurried along behind, her feet tired and her face set with the effort of keeping up.

The Trubble-Bubble eased towards them, smooth and silent.

'Uncle Rick!' Brin said again, pulling at the man's arm. But it was too late. The Trubble-Bubble was alongside them now, and its voice cleared its throat and spoke. 'Hi ho,' it said, 'everything all right?'

Uncle Rick said, 'What—?' and stopped, his face frozen.

'Everything all right?' said the Trubble-Bubble.

Uncle Rick whispered, 'The MPs?' and then answered the Trubble-Bubble. 'Everything all right, chaps!' he said, his voice strained and jolly. 'Everything fine. Bang on.' To Brin, he whispered, 'Weird sort of wagon. Where does its blasted voice come from?'

'Bang on,' repeated the Trubble-Bubble, flatly. It did not change shape—did not extend, as Brin feared it would, its pick-ups. Passing people glanced at the Bubble and the people round it. They looked, and looked away, not wanting to get involved.

The Trubble-Bubble said, 'Bang on,' again, tonelessly: then, 'Well, then, everything's fine. Have a good time.' But it did not move away. There was a pause.

'Lots of things happening tonight,' said the Trubble-Bubble. 'Music in the Centre. Athletics meeting, too. Lots of things to do and see.' It was making time, talking for the sake of talking. Brin knew why. The policemen inside were making their report, getting their instructions—

A flock of pedalec riders came weaving through the crowds. Silvery bells jingled cheerfully. 'Hallo,' said the Trubble-Bubble. 'Citizens having fun! Make way for them, you people! That's the way—'

And very softly, as Uncle Rick and the others moved back, the Trubble-Bubble added, 'Not you, Brin. Come here.'

The pedalecs glittered and whirred past, cutting off Brin from the others. 'Yes?' he said to the Trubble-Bubble.

'Orders for you. Orders from above. Get them back. Take those people back to the Scenario. Those are your *orders*. You understand?'

'Yes.'

'Do it now. Don't waste time. We'll be watching. *They'll* be watching. Better obey, and fast.'

'All right.'

'For your own good,' the Trubble-Bubble said, and— the pedalecs were all gone now—glided away.

Brin stood still, trying to think. 'For your own good': perhaps. But for their good?—for Uncle Rick, Mavis, Brian, Mrs Mossop? Would it be good for them to take them back to the Scenario?

Brian said, 'What was that car thing saying to you?'

'Nothing. Going on about the entertainments,' Brin said, still trying to think.

Brian said, 'What a super car! What a super place!' He looked about him, excitedly. 'What was that about entertainments?' he said.

'Entertainments?' said Uncle Rick. 'Good show! Let's go places and do things! Where shall we go? The athletics? The music? What do you fancy?'

Brin thought, Yes—let's go somewhere. Anywhere.

81

The Seniors can't hurt us while we're all together, out in the open, among the people. But once we're alone, back in the Scenario, they've got us where they want us—

'Athletics!' Brian said, his face alight with expectation.

'No, music!' said Mavis.

'How do you vote, Mrs Mossop?' Uncle Rick said.

'I like music,' she said. 'If it's nice music. I like nice music.' She was out of place and knew it, Brin could see. Worse, she was suspicious. She was looking hard at the strangely-dressed people of the strange, scintillating, light-flooded world.

'Brin?' said Uncle Rick. 'What's your vote?'

'Athletics,' Brin said. Two for Athletics, two for Music—which meant that seconds would be wasted coming to a final decision. And every second might count, Brin knew. They must not go back to the Scenario.

'So I've got the casting vote, it seems,' Uncle Rick said, smiling. 'It's up to me. Right. Tell you what we'll do— we'll go to both!'

Mavis danced round him, saying, 'Yes! Super! Both! Athletics first, then the music. Or the other way round. I don't care! But let's do both!'

'All right, Mrs Mossop?' Uncle Rick said, gallantly.

'A nice cup of tea,' she said. 'That's what I could do with . . . '

A nice cup of tea! Brin thought. I wonder what she'd make of the drinks *we* drink, and the places we drink them? Aloud, he said, 'They'll do tea at the sports place, won't they? They're bound to have a café or restaurant—'

To himself, he said, 'Yes, the Sports Centre. That would be the safest. Fewer people, all those Activity Rooms and changing rooms and corridors and walkways . . . We could get lost in the Sports Centre.'

Aloud, he said, 'Uncle Rick, I know where the Sports Centre is! Let's go!'

Uncle Rick stared at Brin, puzzled. 'Come off it, old lad! How could you know?'

'I—I saw a sign,' Brin said. 'It pointed that way . . .' To avoid explanations, he began to walk away purposefully. They followed him. He avoided the moving pavements, knowing that the Trubble-Bubbles would spot them most easily there. He wove through the crowds, choosing the places where the bright lights cast their darkest shadows.

The others seemed happy to follow his lead. Brin heard Uncle Rick's cheerful voice telling Mavis and Brian, 'I was knocked for a loop when that car thing came up! Thought it was the MPs! Mind you, I've got my leave pass—everything in order, spot-on—but you never know, I mean, I could be recalled at a moment's notice. After all, there's a war on. Though you'd hardly credit it, looking at this place . . .'

They reached the Sports Centre and Brin, suddenly sick, remembered the girl at the entrance. She would be there, or someone like her, to check ID bands. But then he remembered a side exit. Did the door work only one way? He gulped and pushed the door. It opened and they pushed through, Uncle Rick still talking, Mavis still hanging on his arm, her laughing face turned to him, Brian still wide-eyed and ready for anything.

'Are you sure we can get a cup of tea here?' said Mrs Mossop, looking anxiously about her at the fused-glass walls, the silently moving stairs of the escalators, the luminous panels of light. 'Don't *look* like the sort of place they'd serve tea . . .' she said.

Brin forced energy into his voice and movements. 'Come on, come on!' he shouted. 'Follow me! Come on, Mrs Mossop!'

He pushed her on to an escalator. It took them up, as he knew it would, to the long, blank corridors encircling the Centre. Passages and doorways led off to the various

Activities, each labelled with a lit symbol sign. Brin did not want them to look too closely—to see the strangeness of everything. He almost ran down the empty corridors, making the rest keep up with him. 'Tea!' he shouted. 'Nice cup of tea for Mrs Mossop! Whoopee!' He clowned and waved his arms, feeling his left armpit itch.

He managed to break away from the rest completely, running well ahead, jumping in the air and bringing his heels together, yodelling and whooping, behaving like a happy madman. He wanted to get to a refreshments room—an empty one. He had to make sure it was empty before the others caught up with him.

He pushed open the door of the same room he had used when he last visited the Sports Centre—that was the time he met the pleasant couple. He looked inside. Warm, soft lights; warm, soft seats; the servery, clean and welcoming; and it was empty! They were safe. Safe for minutes, a half hour, even an hour!

'Come on!' he called, over his shoulder. 'In here! It's great! Come in here!'

Smiling and chattering and joking, they entered. 'I'll get drinks and things!' Brin said, and turned his back on them so that no one could see the terrified anxiety on his face.

Soon, he knew, someone would say, 'Don't you need some money?'—but money was obsolete.

Soon, Mrs Mossop would say, 'Oo, I don't fancy *that*, are you sure they don't have a nice cup of tea?' Tea was obsolete too.

Soon, the viddy screens on the walls would light with advertisements, news summaries, entertainment flashes— all of them alien, all impossible to explain, all belonging to a time years ahead of their time . . .

It was hopeless but he had to go on with the play. He pressed buttons and let the servery serve him. Frujuice, Blend, Fiz, Chocmalt . . . the beautiful, colourful, hygienic, disposable beakers nestled in the clever, hygienic, colourful trays. 'And a Kolamint!' cooed the automatic voice from the automatic dispenser. Fortunately they were talking too loud to hear the voice. But Uncle Rick would no doubt offer money to pay when Brin brought the drinks to the table. Brin would have to take the coins and pretend to feed them into the machine.

But Mrs Mossop would still want her nice cup of tea . . .

He began to carry the loaded tray—remembering just in time not to put it on the Choot, the automatic delivery system—to the table. His hands shook and the liquids jiggled in their beakers.

As he reached the table, a door in the dimness at the other end of the long room opened and closed silently. A girl came in. Brin could make out her long hair and long bare legs. The whiteness of her brief sports outfit was almost luminous in the shaded warm light. Brin could not see her face, it could be anyone. It could even be Madi!

He knew it was Madi when he saw the girl begin to make the Sign of Politeness—then check herself. She turned the Sign into a vague wave of the hand. Her voice—it was Madi's voice, there could be no mistaking it—murmured a vague, friendly sound of greeting.

Brin put the tray down just in time. Another moment and the drinks would have spilled: his hands were shaking uncontrollably.

Madi came closer. Brin cursed her, silently. Uncle Rick stared at Madi's legs and made a little whistling sound. Brin saw his teeth gleaming as he smiled under his big, wispy moustache.

Madi walked past them to the servery and pressed buttons. Now her back was to Brin and the others. Brin felt

85

he was choking. Madi had followed them, found them. So, no doubt, Tello and the other Seniors knew where he was. The Trubble-Bubbles were outside, waiting. Not long now before it was all over, Brin knew.

Mrs Mossop nervously sipped her drink. 'It's very nice I'm sure, but you'd have thought they'd have tea . . . ' Uncle Rick tried not to stare at Madi. Mavis and Brian, silent for a moment when Madi came in, were talking again—'Mine's super, like an orange and lemon and pineapple all mixed up!'—'Let's swap, you have a sip of mine, I'll have a sip of yours!'—'Only a sip, no gulping!' Madi still stood with her back to them.

A viddy screen on the wall lit up. The usual mellow little chimes sounded, politely. A written message appeared on the screen:

ATENSHUN PLEAZ!

Madi turned, smiled and called, 'I think you've left one of your drinks behind . . . Would someone like to come and get it?'

Uncle Rick began to get up from his seat, but Brin muttered, 'No, I'll do it. My fault.' He went over to Madi. The screens now flashed the word—

URJENT!

Brian giggled and said, 'Can't spell!'

Brin stood by Madi. His voice would hardly work. 'Yes?' he croaked.

She smiled and held out a drink to Brin. Speaking loudly enough to be overheard, she said, 'This drink isn't mine, so I suppose it must be yours.' She smiled again and continued, speaking very softly, 'You were told to get them back to the Scenario. You didn't do it. All right. Now you can have it either way—nice or nasty. The nice way is to get them back—'

86

'But I can't just—they haven't finished their drinks—I've no reason to make them go—' Brin said, lamely.

'We've thought of that. Watch the viddy.'

The viddy screens now displayed

URJENT!

LEEV THE SENTER!

UNEXPLODED BOM

Even as Brin watched, the spelling changed

URGENT!

LEAVE THE CENTRE!

UNEXPLODED BOMB

The screen began to flash the message. The chimes sounded continuously, urgently.

'The nice way is to get them back,' Madi repeated. 'Do it any way you like. We have a cab outside. Get them into it.'

'And the nasty way?' Brin said, miserably. 'No, don't tell me. You'd destroy them here, wouldn't you? Kill them in front of each other?'

'We wouldn't do it noisily,' Madi said, smiling brightly. 'But we'd do it. We'd start with Mrs Mossop. She should be dead by now anyway.'

Brin said, 'All right. I'll get them back to the Scenario.'

'It's a blue taxi with a white stripe,' said Madi.

The screens said

LEAVE THE BUILDING

IMMEDIATELY

TRANSPORT IS PROVIDED

Brin rejoined his party. 'Rotten swizz!' Mavis said, gulping down her drink as she stood up.

'Jerry ruins everything,' Brian grumbled.

'Better get out, and sharpish,' Uncle Rick said, helping

Mrs Mossop to her feet. To Brin, he said, 'Lead on, MacDuff!'

Brin led them along the corridors, through the exit door, to the street. A blue taxi with a white stripe slid like a fish towards them. 'In you get!' said the driver. 'Can't tell when that bomb might go off!'

Before he could prevent it, Uncle Rick had bundled him and the others inside the cab.

Minutes later, they fumbled their way through the dark place that represented the hall of the old house: and were back in 1940, back in the kitchen, back in the Scenario.

Trapped.

'I don't care!' Mavis said. Her eyes still sparkled, particularly when she looked at Uncle Rick. She whirled about the kitchen and scullery, filling a kettle, getting milk from the icebox, putting out cups and saucers—yet somehow wherever she was she always seemed near Uncle Rick.

'*I* care!' Brian said. 'Rotten swizz! Especially for Uncle Rick. Just when we'd chanced on that super place—and everything set for a terrific evening—that's when the stupid rotten *war* has to come in and spoil everything!'

'I don't care!' Uncle Rick said. 'Stop moaning! Here we are together, and I've got forty-eight hours' leave, and the kettle's on—and I've met Mavis and Brian and Mrs Mossop for the first time . . . and seen my nephew Brin once again—so are we downhearted?'

He cocked a hand comically behind his ear to receive the answer, 'NO-O-O!' Brian and Mavis shouted their NO! lustily. Mrs Mossop giggled her 'No!' then said 'Tsk, tsk' and needlessly rearranged all the cups and saucers, smiling to herself. When Uncle Rick called her the Good Fairy of the Teapot she said, 'Oh, go along with you' and pushed his shoulder with her hand. Her spectacles seemed to twinkle.

Brin was silent: because Brin knew. Not everything, but more than enough. He knew that some sort of curtain was to descend over the Scenario, and the play, and the players. There had to be an ending: most probably a violent ending. He wondered why he was not more afraid.

He knew that Uncle Rick, now the central figure of the play, was an impossible lie. He could not exist, yet— 'Ludo!' Uncle Rick shouted. 'Haven't played it for a hundred years! Ludo! Imagine! When I was a kid, I always bagsed be red—'

'You can be red now,' Mavis said. 'Here you are!' She twisted the board round on the carpet in front of the kitchen range so that the red base faced Uncle Rick. 'I don't mind what colour I am,' she said.

'But you'll have to take green!' Brian said. 'You hate being green!'

'No I don't. I *like* green . . . ' She put Uncle Rick's pieces in place for him.

He said, 'Right! Just watch me! Just watch me, that's all! Six after six! Never fails! King of the six-shooters, that's your Uncle Rick!'

Brin slowly set out his yellow pieces and made himself remember the scene around him. The kitchen range, with its name ALBION on the oven door and the words PEACE & PLENTY below, in smaller cast-iron letters. The smell of the range's glowing coals, and their little private clinkings and tickings and sudden minor landslides. The kettle, on the hob now, singing breathily to itself. The faded, ugly pattern of the carpet on which he knelt, with its little black-brown holes made by burning fragments of coal. The creaking of the wicker chair, where Mrs Mossop sat, knitting, her face creased and shining. The familiar ugliness of the kitchen, with the blackout like a big wall over the main window. Blackie, half asleep on Mavis's school scarf which she had thrown on the lid of the gingery-brown icebox. Worn lino, chipped chairs, oilcloth and ironing, fluffy dust on the flex from which hung the glaring electric-light bulb in the middle of the ceiling. The sparkle of the cups, the smell of the tea.

All to go soon, he knew. How soon? How would the end come?

'Six!' yelled Brian. 'One!—two!—three!—four!—five!—six! And *another* throw, *if* you please! . . . One, two, three, four . . . And that gets me safely home, thank you very much! Beat that, Uncle Rick!'

'Enough of this!' Uncle Rick growled, ferociously. 'Give me that dice.' He rolled his eyes, scowled, waggled his moustache fiercely and shook the dice in his clenched fist, near to his ear. 'Six!' he said to the dice. 'You hear me? Six! Come on, come on, *come on* . . . '

'Come on!' said the Senior Elect, impatiently. He tapped the horseshoe table with his old-fashioned ballpoint. 'We will have no more recriminations and post-mortems and examinations of what has been done. I am asking you what *will* be done. Tello?'

Tello, his face troubled, said, 'I think . . . I think we must keep on with the experiment. We simply can't throw it all away now.'

The horse-faced woman Senior said, 'Simply! He says, "Simply"! There is nothing simple about what is happening. It is complicated, difficult, even dangerous—'

'Dangerous?' said the Chinese-looking Senior in her high, pleasant voice. 'I do not see a danger. I see a mystery, but where is the danger?'

'The mystery is the danger,' replied the horse-faced Senior.

'If there is a mystery,' said the Senior Elect, tapping his ballpoint faster, 'will someone please explain it and solve it. If there is a danger, we will face it. But let us do it promptly! Tello?'

Tello sighed, massively. 'We are a scientific race,' he began. 'We rely on science to provide our needs and advance our purposes. The Reborn programme is typical of our approach. Reborns are the scientific answer to a problem caused by a scientific disaster.'

'Please, get *on*!' said the Senior Elect.

But Tello continued to speak slowly, almost tiredly. 'From the moment we constructed the first Reborn, we became Gods, creators of life. We reached a godlike summit, through science. We knew what we did; we knew how we did it. We understood, completely, the nature of our achievement . . .

'But now, we find that the creatures we created can do something more than us. Without science—without our huge store of knowledge, built up over the centuries—the creatures we made, mere Reborn children, have outdone us. They too have made a living creature! This Uncle Rick! . . .

'And they've made him from nothing! No genes, no chromosomes, no electric currents, no Genetic Recoders, for them! They merely said, "Let there be life!"—and there was life.'

The Senior Elect rubbed his nose disgustedly. 'The purpose of this meeting is to decide what to do about this—Uncle Rick. Granted—he is scientifically impossible. Granted—his existence contradicts the basis of our whole civilization. So what *do* we do about him, and his creators?'

'Terminate their lives,' said the horse-faced Senior.

'Terminate them?' said a quiet Senior. A man who seldom spoke, a quiet, small man, leader of the team that made the Reborns. 'I don't think you mean what you say. Terminate? I'm not sure . . . '

'Why not kill them?' snapped the Senior Elect.

'I was going to say,' said the quiet Senior, 'that I'm not sure we *can* kill them. Oh, I know, we made them so we should be able to terminate them. But this Uncle Rick: he may not *consent* to death. He may refuse to be killed by our sort of science!'

'He is flesh and blood,' said the horse-faced Senior. 'Flesh and blood can be destroyed.'

'And a spirit?' said the quiet Senior. 'Can we be sure of destroying spirits, too?'

The Chinese-looking Senior said, 'But this is absurd! Now we are talking of ghosts and myths and bogeymen! Surely if you kill the flesh-and-blood body, you kill the person!'

Speaking almost to himself, the quiet Senior said, 'Donald Duck.'

The Senior Elect sighed elaborately and said, 'I beg your pardon? Did I understand you to say ''Donald Duck''?'

'Oh, and Charlie Chaplin,' said the quiet Senior. 'And so many others—the great names—Shakespeare and Dickens and Bach. I can't remember all of them offhand. Hardly my field. Buddha, Muhammed, Jesus Christ . . . '

'If there is a point, please get to it,' said the Senior Elect, icily.

'The point? Well, it is obvious, surely. The centuries pass, yet these people are all alive. They still live, in a sense. Our children still laugh at Donald Duck, all these years after he was created—'

'The point!' almost shouted the Senior Elect.

'But he has come to the point,' said Tello. 'He's saying that the parts of a person that are *not* flesh and blood can live on indefinitely. As witness the founders of religions, the great artists—even Donald Duck, who was never flesh and blood, never anything more than a series of funny drawings. Yet there is a force of the spirit, a life force, that survives—'

'Where is the danger in that?' said the horse-faced Senior.

The quiet Senior replied. 'Strength,' he said. 'Such forces are strong.'

'We are strong! Our science is strong!' said the Chinese-looking Senior.

'But also weak,' said the quiet Senior. 'It was our science, remember, that nearly put an end to our human race.'

'But then we created Reborns—from Science!'

Tello said, 'And the Reborns created a raw, natural human being. Without science! How did they do it? That is the mystery. Will they continue to do it? That is the danger. For if their humans, who can breed, prove stronger and more effective than our infertile humans, one day there may be no place left for us on this planet!'

There was a long silence. The Senior Elect broke it by throwing down his ballpoint on the shining surface of the great desk. 'Enough!' he shouted. 'I will tolerate no more of this! These circular arguments that end where they begin and begin where they end! This talk of spirits and mysteries and threats!—' His voice cracked and for a moment became an old man's quaverings. He clenched his hands; set his mouth; and spoke again, quietly.

'We must act,' he said. 'Act now, on the facts. Fact: the Reborns have broken out of the Scenario. Fact: they have created a being who, some of you seem to believe, might threaten our own future. Which leads to three simple, easily answered questions on which I demand your votes and decisions.

'First, the Experiment. Shall it continue, or shall we end it?

'Second, the Reborns. If we decide to remove them from the experiment, do we permit them to continue to exist—or do we terminate them?

'Third, the creature the Reborns created—this Uncle Rick. Does he live or does he die? And please do not tell me,' he said viciously to the quiet Senior, 'that Rick cannot be killed because I say he can . . .

'Those are the questions on which you will vote,' he continued. 'When I have your joint decision, it will be acted on immediately. Other matters—what to do with the Reborn children if you decide that they may live, and so on—will be decided in due course.

'But now you will vote, without further delay, on the three major questions. On those questions and those questions only.'

The Senior Elect gave the Sign of Politeness. The Seniors responded, then placed their hands on the surface of the table. Under their fingertips lay two flat tablets, flush with the table. A minute pressure, an invisible movement of the muscles of a finger, was enough to press down one of the two tablets. For the fingers of the right hand, Yes. For the fingers of the left, No.

'You are all ready?' said the Senior Elect.

There was a murmur of assent—then Tello said, 'You have not mentioned the boy Brin! Surely we must decide about him too?'

The Senior Elect raised his eyebrows. 'I cannot see why,' he said. 'Surely he can wait? Isn't his a . . . a rather separate case?'

Tello opened his mouth but decided not to speak. He too lowered his hands until they rested on the shining table, over the two neat, flat, fatal tablets.

'Superman!' Uncle Rick cried, shaking his head admiringly.

94

'That's what you are, Brin! How does he do it?' he asked Mavis and Brian. 'I mean, he wasn't even trying! Not with us at all! Chucking the dice down any old how—yet there he is, home and dry, while I've still got two men stuck at base—'

'I've got three!' Mavis groaned. 'Brin sent two of mine back, and Uncle Rick caught me just when I was getting this one home . . . ' she groaned dramatically and leaned towards Uncle Rick, who patted her head and grinned at her.

Brin forced himself to make the right sounds and faces. He'd won two games of Ludo in a row, barely knowing he had been playing. 'Superior talent,' Brin said. 'Greater intellect! I'm just cleverer than anyone else in the world, that's why I win—'

'Cleverer?' said Brian. 'Luckier, you mean! Honestly, the way Brin managed to keep out of my way when I was right on his tail—it just wasn't *natural*!'

Brin thought, Not natural? Not natural . . . cleverer . . . greater intellect . . . Superman.

Did the words add up to something? His high IQ. His fantastic memory. Were they natural? And if they weren't, what was the connection between his superman status and his itching armpit? To hide his face and his thoughts, he poured himself more tea.

Mrs Mossop said, 'You don't want to drink that, that's dishwater! If you want tea, you stir your stumps and make fresh. We could all do with another cup, I dare say.'

Mavis said, 'Wait a tick. Quiet!' and held a hand to her ear. A long way away, the sirens started, rising and falling like banshee voices.

'Air-raid warning!' Brian said, disgustedly. 'Which means that we can't get out of here, now. We're stuck.'

'That Hitler,' said Mrs Mossop. 'Well, I suppose I'd better do the ironing, then.'

Brin said—hoping Madi, behind the dresser, could hear, wishing he could see her pretty, healthy face shadowed with anger and frustration—'Oh! Don't go near that light by your table, Mrs Mossop! I touched it tonight,' he lied, 'and it gave me a shock! It ought to be mended!' To himself, he said, 'They're going to kill us all one way or another, I suppose. But at least we can all go together.'

Uncle Rick said, 'Ought to mend it right away, you know! Let's have a look!' He went to the switch, pulling a fountain pen out of his tunic pocket. With the pen, he flicked the tumbler switch—

There was a blue flash and a deafening, smashing bang . . . The switch exploded from the wall, rocketed across the room and smashed itself to pieces on the kitchen range. The wall smoked. It was blackened by the explosion round the switch. Uncle Rick repeated in a stunned voice, 'I *say*! . . . I *say*! . . . I *say*!' and stared at the gnarled, melted stump he held; it was all that remained of his fountain pen.

Brin began to shake with a laughter that he couldn't control, laughter like a volcano inside him. Brian was shaking and heaving too. 'But look at my fountain pen!' Uncle Rick said. 'It's been written off!'

'Pen . . . written off!' Brian said. 'That's funny, you know! Pen, written off!'

And then they were all laughing, Brin and Mavis and Brian and Mrs Mossop, laughing uncontrollably. Uncle Rick too. The kettle boiled over noisily, Blackie the cat said, 'Mrr-aow!' and gazed at them owlishly and they laughed and laughed and laughed, out of control.

Much nearer now, the sirens swooped and moaned. Brin's laughter actually hurt him, his sides ached and his mind said, So that's it: we're to be destroyed in an air-raid. Very soon now. But aloud, he said—his words broken into meaningless sounds by the racking, choking, glorious

96

laughter—'Satisfied, Madi? Happy now, Tello? Because I'm happy! I don't care any more! You can't hurt any of us now!'

For the explosion had somehow set off another instantaneous explosion in his own mind. In that crashing split second, he had suddenly realized the truth about himself, a truth so awful and fundamental that it, too, had to be laughed at. The great truth included the discoveries that his whole life had been a lie—and even that false life was shortly to end.

He even knew, now, why his left armpit itched. And that small revelation made him laugh all the more helplessly as, above the sound of the sirens, the sullen, pulsing, mumble of the approaching bombers was heard.

Tello's expression was even blacker than his skin. 'You cannot do this!' he thundered, raising his white-gowned arms shoulder high until he took the posture of a man crucified.

The Senior Elect flinched, but then steadied his gaze and looked back at Tello. 'We can,' he said. 'We will.'

'The votes are cast,' said the Chinese-looking Senior, her voice as light and charming as ever. But she averted her eyes when she spoke.

'But it is savage—stupid—brutal—wasteful!' cried Tello, unconsciously echoing the words once used by Brin.

'It will be done,' said the Senior Elect. 'It is being done. The vote has been taken. They die.'

The quiet Senior stood on his feet, his face grey. '*I* voted that they live!' he said. 'Let it be known how *I* voted!'

'We are not interested,' said the Senior Elect. 'Indeed,' he added, scornfully, 'we do not hear you. We *must* not

97

hear you. The vote is always a secret vote. We do not ask and must not know how any one Senior voted.'

'I think you know how I voted,' said Tello.

The quiet Senior looked despairingly at Tello, then sank back slowly into his seat. 'It is not . . . not *scientific* . . . ' he complained, almost in a whimper.

'Cruel, stupid, wasteful, inhuman!' cried Tello, alone and defiant on the floor of the chamber.

'Inhuman?' said the Senior Elect. 'Ah! With that word you make some sense. Inhuman, certainly. Mavis, a Reborn. Brian, a Reborn. Mrs Mossop, a Reborn. Uncle Rick—well, let us say a figment of the imagination—an effort of will disguised as a human.'

'And the boy Brin?' demanded Tello.

'Enough!' said the Senior Elect. 'It is nearly time. Tomorrow, we have serious business to discuss. The matter before us tonight will very shortly be completed. Over and done with, Tello. Never to be discussed again, you understand?'

He rose to his feet. The others—all but Tello—also arose. The Senior Elect made the Sign of Politeness. The others—all but Tello—responded. All but Tello left the chamber of the Council of the Elect, their robes hissing gently on the pictured floor.

And Tello stood alone.

The bombs, still distant, whistled down, whistling out of tune with each other. 'Wheeee!' they went, on descending notes; 'CRUMP!' they went as they hit their targets and shook the mean kitchen of the Scenario.

Brin saw Mrs Mossop's face turn yellowish beneath the brown: saw her bite her lower lip, then catch herself doing it and make herself stop. 'That Hitler,' she said, 'I'd give him Hitler . . . '

A play, a recording, a stage set! thought Brin. If only I could tell her, and the others! Lies, lies! But they would not believe me. And it would not help them. And there isn't time.

The drone of the bombers was very near now. The unsynchronized motors growled, 'Rrrrum . . . rrrum . . . RRRUM' as if a great coarse millwheel were turning in the sky, grinding lives between broken teeth. Blackie the cat laid his ears back and jumped smoothly from the top of the icebox; then burrowed into the gap beneath it. '*He* knows what's good for him!' said Mrs Mossop, affectionately grumbling. 'Imp of Satan!'

If only I could tell them it's all right, Brin thought. Tell them that nothing is real—not the bombers nor anything else. But would it help? They must still die.

Suddenly, shatteringly, nearby anti-aircraft guns fired. CRUMP! CRUMP—CRUMP! Mavis said, 'Oh . . . ' and moved, without meaning to, towards Uncle Rick; then, self-conscious, moved away again.

But he reached out a long arm and drew her to him so that her head was against his chest. 'Don't desert a fellow!' he said. 'I can't stand bangs! Get the wind-up even when someone pulls a Christmas cracker! Need moral support! Did I tell you how I got my medal? Would you like to hear? Well, I'll tell you . . . ' He began a story about being frightened out of his skin by a bang inside his aircraft. He talked without a pause, his arm round Mavis, protecting her, talking faster and faster, to hold her attention, shield her from fear.

Outside, there was a whistling shriek, very loud—and a horrifying smash that made the kitchen jump and judder and leak dust from the ceiling. The dust came down and down through the shaking air, bright round the central lamp, indistinct elsewhere . . .

'. . . I was so frightened by the bang that I jumped out

of my skin!—Went straight up, straight through the canopy of my aircraft, crash-bang, right up into the sky!' Uncle Rick told Mavis.

'What happened then?' Brian said, grinning as he flicked dust from his face. Brian, too, now stood very close to Uncle Rick.

'Well, there was this Jerry, an ME109, just above me, you see. And somehow I grabbed his tailwheel! And poor Jerry had to fly with me hanging on behind—but the extra weight wasn't what he'd reckoned with, so he started looping the loop . . . Looooping the loooop!'

More bombs fell, a whole stick of them. Not so near this time. Streets away. But Brin saw the crack in the ceiling, over the dresser, zip and spread. A fine trickle of plaster dust became a steady stream, like the thread of sand in an hour-glass, trickling down and down. The room shook again. The trickle became thick and threatening.

'Table!' Brian muttered and pushed Mrs Mossop under the ironing table. But Uncle Rick did not stop his story. Even as he pushed Mavis under the table he was always talking, always grinning.

The crack in the ceiling widened. The ceiling sagged in the corner, very slightly at first, but then another bomb fell and the room shook again and the whole triangular corner of the plaster ceiling silently hinged downwards. Only the top of the high dresser kept it in position. No one else noticed. They were listening to Uncle Rick.

'. . . Going round and round like a catherine-wheel, this ME109 was! Faster and faster! So fast that the Jerry pilot bust his straps and went hurtling out through the canopy! Centrifugal force, you see! Very powerful . . . '

A Reborn! Brin thought. *That's what I am! I should have guessed earlier. The itching should have told me. I wonder how long ago they made me? It can't have been long. Otherwise the pinpricks in my armpit would have healed more completely, they wouldn't still itch from being so new. Fool, why didn't I guess? A Reborn, just like the others! No, but not like them. I wasn't made from the rags and bones of their time! I'm one of the people of today, my body is smaller, I belong to the new, sterile breed of superhumans. And I suppose I was given a super Sleeper to make me super-intelligent, super-useful for the great experiment, super-everything. And now I'm superseded, superfluous, superannuated. I'm a dead loss, or just about to become one . . .*

Bombs began screaming. The screams were the loudest yet. Uncle Rick paused and looked up at the ceiling. There was sweat as well as dust on his forehead. Mavis clutched his arm—her hands were white and clawed—and said, 'Go on, Uncle Rick! Go on!' He heard her above the screaming of the bombs. He put his head on one side, waggled his moustache, and told her, 'So the ME109 whipped right round, turned head-over-heels—and flung me off the tailwheel! And you'd never guess where I landed up!' Now he had to shout.

'Go on!' she said—she too had to shout above the screaming of the bombs—'Don't stop! It's so funny!' Her mouth was a clenched hole in the terrified mask of her face, her fingers clasped his sleeve.

'So I landed *in the seat of the ME109!*' shouted Uncle Rick, triumphantly. 'Flew it back to base, I did!' Uncle Rick seized Brin and flung him at the table: 'Get under! Quick!'

Screaming! The bomb's screaming was intolerably loud—Brin only wanted it to land and explode and blow them all to smithereens, then it would all be over and finished—why did it have to take so long? Had they got the recordings wrong? The bombers were only a recording, none of it was real, only the end part was real, the last explosions, the deaths—

There was no room for Uncle Rick. He was squatting

101

by the table, waving his arms, finishing his story, shouting it, bellowing it. 'So I flew the Jerry plane back to base and they gave me a medal!' he yelled. *'Enormous gong! Captured enemy aircraft single-handed!* Brave Uncle Rick!'

'Yes!' Mavis shouted, reaching out an arm, curling it round his neck. 'Oh, yes, Uncle Rick!' And Brian had taken Uncle Rick's other hand, holding it tightly, looking into his eyes, making himself smile. And Mrs Mossop was trying to smile too, her lips were moving and her head nodding as if to say, 'Yes, yes, yes!' And Uncle Rick was outside the table yet holding them all together, smiling right through their eyes and getting inside them, telling them 'Yes!'

The bomb exploded.

The city quivered. Riders stopped their pedalecs and looked around them. 'What was that?'

'I don't know. Sounded like an explosion.'

'An explosion? But that's impossible. We don't have explosions . . .'

'We do. Remember years ago, when that electric feeder went up? That was a bang.'

'What's an electric feeder?'

'I don't know. Something to do with the city's power supply, I suppose. But it went up. Bang.'

'Well, everything's quiet now.'

The riders remounted their machines. A Trubble-Bubble glided by, its voice cosy and cheerful. 'Everything's fine,' it said. 'Enjoy yourselves. Everything's fine.'

The pedalec riders rode off. The night sky glittered with signs and coloured reflections from the tall, glassy buildings. If you looked hard, you could see the stars of the firmament beyond the transparent dome covering the city. But the stars were dim against the flashing signs, the towering, gleaming walls.

'The bomb has exploded!' said the Senior Elect as the Council Chamber of the Elect quivered very slightly.

'I know,' said Tello, bitterly. 'I felt the force of the explosion. So did *they*. Only they felt it rather more strongly.'

The horse-faced woman Senior said, 'Very well arranged. A well-contained explosion. We felt a mere tremor here. I think congratulations are in order.' She bowed her long face on its long neck to the quiet Senior. He had arranged the explosion. He shook his head angrily and averted his face from her.

'A mere tremor,' said Tello. 'And for *them*, a white-hot inferno: flesh torn from bones, blood turned to vapour, brains mashed to pulp. Oh, yes! Congratulations are in order!'

The Senior Elect said, 'That will do,' and touched a button under the horseshoe desk. A wall lit up with moving pictures. They showed the people in the streets of the city. Heads turned, eyes looked about, groups of puzzled people formed and dispersed, talking to each other, asking questions. But soon, the groups broke up. Shoulders shrugged, mouths smiled. People went on their way.

'They hardly noticed it,' said the Chinese-looking Senior, brightly. 'But I suppose we ought to make a news announcement, all the same? Just to set everyone's mind at rest?'

'Oh, yes,' said the Senior Elect. 'Say something. Anything will do. What did we say last time? When we had to dispense with those agitators, those Dissidents? It was some time ago, I don't remember.'

103

'Something about an electric feeder,' said the Chinese-looking Senior, smiling.

'Well, use that again,' said the Senior Elect. 'Electric feeder. By the by, what *is* an electric feeder?'

He turned his head enquiringly to the quiet Senior; but once again, there was no reply other than an angry turn of the head.

The Senior Elect said, 'Ah, well. Yes, I think we may congratulate ourselves. The matter is concluded. Ended.'

Tello stared at the Senior Elect and raised an eyebrow questioningly. 'Ended?' he said. 'Perhaps . . . '

The bomb exploded.

To Brin, its fall had been endlessly drawn-out—an eternity of stretched split-seconds.

The explosion, too, was another eternity. He saw, as if by a lightning flash, the dingy kitchen heave, lift itself upwards, and the dusty light-flex snake, and the glass of an electric lamp crinkle and collapse inwards—perhaps he even saw the white-hot filament dim and die and its tiny spiderweb snap its threads (but, yes!, he did see Mavis, her eyes wide to receive the beam of pure will from Uncle Rick, the will to live).

He saw the walls judder and jar and crack, and the china plates hop—some of them broke as if hit by invisible bullets—on the bending shelves of the dresser, and the shelves leap from their brackets and catapult towards him, splitting apart to show clean white wood under the old, sad paint (and, yes!, he saw Brian's eyes, turned away for just one moment from Uncle Rick's, looking to Mrs Mossop, who still had the forced smile printed on her worn brown face, who still stared trustingly into the face of Uncle Rick).

He saw the ceiling fall, the walls rush towards him,

the chairs spinning in a hurricane wind. He saw the dumb, blackleaded face of the kitchen range split, and the iron word ALBION suddenly very big, flying towards him, smashing through the leg of the table (and, yes! he saw Uncle Rick's face—no, it was his eyes, it was his eyes that mattered—sure and smiling and saying 'Yes!').

He saw Blackie, the cat, eyes ablaze, pink mouth open to show white, curved, defiant teeth.

He saw the ceiling and the wall smash down on the brown icebox: it bulged and splintered and flattened.

He saw white flame and purple flame, flying glass and spurting dust.

He saw his own flesh tear from his fingers. (But, yes! He had been born of a rag, a bone, a hank of hair, and Uncle Rick's eyes told him that a Reborn could be reborn!)

He shouted 'LIVE!'—and died.

Madi, her pretty face sulky and withdrawn, said, 'I don't know what you are talking about. *I* don't hear voices.'

Tello laughed, lazily, and said, 'Perhaps I should take more exercise.'

She said, 'Yes. Perhaps you should. *Voices!*' She walked away from the big black man, disliking him. Before—but before *what?*—she had liked him better than any of the other Seniors, liked his massiveness, his deep, easy voice, the feeling of security and certainty he gave people. Now he made her uneasy—even angry. Everything seemed somehow different, ever since—since *what?*

Annoyed with herself, annoyed with thoughts of Tello, she took the walkway and headed for the Sports Centre. She tried to concentrate on the bustle around her, the people, the signs, the buildings. But all the time, her uneasiness nagged her. What had she to be uneasy about?

She had been quite all right before—before *what*? Since *what*? 'All right, I'll admit it,' she told herself: 'Before those Reborns. After those Reborns. But why bother about them? They're finished now.'

As for this talk of voices, hearing voices . . . Nonsense! '*I* don't hear them!' she said, under her breath. A man next to her on the walkway said, 'Pardon?' and she replied, 'Oh, nothing!' and smiled at him, still more annoyed with herself. Hearing voices! It was her own voice that had spoken just now.

She showed her ID band at the Centre, changed in the changing rooms, swam six lengths in the pool, plunging through the artificial salty waves. She felt better. She lay on her back in a corner where the waves were small and gentle and looked at the water spilling over her golden stomach. Much better! She thought, I wonder why more citizens don't come here. It's free, and gorgeous, and makes you feel really alive—

Very loudly in her ear, a voice from nowhere shouted, 'LIVE!'

She swallowed water, floundered, left the pool and stood under a fresh-water shower. The splashing of the water would be too loud to let any voices through, she thought.

She turned the water to cold and let it chill her. 'Cold commonsense,' she murmured. She had not heard a voice. The voice had not shouted 'LIVE!' She was not going to hear the voice again, just when she was falling asleep. It was all nonsense. A trick of the brain.

'*Brain, Brian, Brin,*' her mind said.

'Nonsense!' she shouted and turned the shower water on full. The water roared at her, battered at her, drowning any possibility of hearing the Voices . . .

In the Council Chamber of the Elect, the Senior Elect said,

'Any other business?' His voice was tired. But then, his body was tired. 'You are an old man!' he told himself. 'Soon, you can resign your position as head of the Western Elect, and become a philosopher, a commentator, a distinguished observer, a historian. You deserve your retirement. What did Shakespeare's Othello say? ''I have done the state some service . . . '' Othello, Tello. Perhaps Tello will take my place when I resign. I wish I could like the idea of him sitting in this chair when I am dead—'

'LIVE!' shouted a voice from nowhere, a deafening voice.

The Senior Elect jumped—pulled himself together—and repeated, 'Any other business?' He hardly heard the replies. Voices! He was hearing voices! Time for him to retire . . .

The Chinese-looking Senior, alone in her apartment, made herself tea. A luxury. A treat not known to other people. She, however, had chosen to preserve the old custom, and something of the formality of the oriental ceremony connected with tea-making. Not like the Japanese, of course: that was going too far. But the quiet, meditative, private, personal, gentle ceremony of boiling the water—setting the beautiful chinaware—handling the bamboo spoons—well, it was pleasant. Very pleasant. It put her into a frame of mind that, she knew, belonged to her ancestors. It placed her in another time in history, took her away from a too-crowded present. It conferred a sort of dignity and calm on an overcrowded life—

'LIVE!' the voice shouted.

She flinched, but ignored the voice. She took the bamboo scoop between finger and thumb, so . . . and

107

measured out the fragile tea leaves, so . . . and carefully, gracefully, lifted the little flowered teapot to—

'Tally ho!' said a voice, a laughing, cheerful, young man's voice. 'Brewing up? Wish I could join you, I'm parched! Perhaps I *will* be able to join you—I hope I'm not butting in, didn't see you clearly, can't quite make things out—'

The voice faded. The Chinese-looking Senior sighed, letting out her breath. It was happening more and more often nowadays, hearing the Voices. She finished her private tea ceremony, sat down on the long wide sofa and made herself concentrate on the fragrance of the tea. She turned down the lights so that the low, cool, orderly living-room was illuminated only by one warmly-glowing sphere. She sipped the tea.

In the shadows of the corner, something dark moved. She jerked upright, almost spilling the tea. Two greenish-yellow glints, like eyes. There! It moved again!

She rose to her feet and went to the dark corner. As she had expected, there was nothing there. Nothing at all. She stood, small and neat and determined, inspecting the corner. She thought she heard a sound, a high sound, like the mewing of a cat.

She bent down and looked more intently into the corner—then remembered a nearby light switch and switched on a lamp. Nothing, except dust.

Dust! Slightly shocked, she moved from the corner and walked briskly to the service room, where she touched a little flat switch. A small lilac-coloured machine nosed out of the wall and began to run round the floor. With her toe, the Chinese-looking Senior guided the machine to the dusty corner, where it busily ate dust.

'Wait!' she cried—but too late: before she could stop it the machine got to the print in the dust—

The pawmarks of a cat.

The machine gobbled it up.

'Carried?' said the Senior Elect. 'Good. Carried. We are agreed, then, by a majority vote, to continue with the Reborn programme.'

Tello tried to speak. The Senior Elect raised his hand and silenced him. 'No, Senior Tello. I must forbid you. We know your views. You have put them forcefully and clearly. But the over-riding consideration is the continuance of the human species—'

'No Reborns, no human race!' interrupted the horse-faced Senior, loudly and harshly.

'You know the risks,' Tello said, 'that is all I wanted to say. To remind you, yet again, of the risks.'

'We know the risks of *not* continuing with the Reborn programme,' said the horse-faced Senior, and folded her arms.

The quiet Senior spoke. 'You won't listen to my voice, I suppose,' he began, speaking so quietly that the horse-faced Senior said, 'Can hardly *hear* his voice! Wish he'd speak up!' The quiet Senior cleared his throat and continued, 'As I say, you won't heed my voice, but—are there any *other* voices you should listen to, do you think?'

'Other voices?' said the Seniors.

'Don't know what he's talking about!'

'What voices?'

'Has he been *hearing voices*? Well, well!'

The indignant chorus died down. The quiet Senior said, 'You have answered my question. There are no other voices you need listen to. Of course not. I am perfectly satisfied. Thank you.'

There was a blank silence. At last the Senior Elect said,

'Yes. Well. Turning to the question of the Reborn programme . . .'

'I hear you!' said Tello. His voice was a quiet, velvet rumble. His eyes were closed. He lay on his back in the dark. Outside his bedroom, the city was quiet. Yet he still could not hear the voices properly.

'Go on, go on!' he said to the blackness.

'. . . Don't know where I am half the time!' said Uncle Rick's voice, still cheerful—but Tello could hear the underlying anxiety and doubt. '. . . Ought to rejoin my Squadron, I suppose. But then, they did give me leave. Got another forty-eight hours left. Plenty of time to look up Brin, my nephew. Nice kid, they tell me. Trouble is, I don't really know London. And the blackout doesn't help . . .'

The voice faded. 'Go on!' muttered Tello. But the voice was gone.

Then Brin spoke, 'My armpit itches! I know why. At least, I did know, but I've forgotten. Old Brian doesn't like losing at Ludo, does he? You should have seen his face when I threw that third six!'

Tello lay waiting. Only his lips moved. 'Come on,' he whispered, 'tell me! Come and tell me! I'm listening.'

Suddenly Mavis said, very loudly, 'Blackie! Down! Oo, you are a devil, that's the last of the milk!'

'Go on!' said Tello, but all he could hear was the thump-thump-thump of an iron on an ironing-board.

'Mrs Mossop?' said Tello. But the voices were gone. He sighed, turned over on his side and eventually fell into an uneasy sleep, filled with wild and impossible dreams, and voices calling.

Also in this series

The Eagle of the Ninth
Rosemary Sutcliff
ISBN 0 19 271765 0

The Ninth Legion marched into the mists of northern Britain. And they never came back. Four thousand men disappeared and the Eagle standard was lost. Marcus Aquila, a young Roman officer, needs to find out what happened to his father and the Ninth Legion. He sets out into the unknown territory of the north on a quest so hazardous that no one expects him to return . . .

Outcast
Rosemary Sutcliff
ISBN 0 19 271766 9

Sickness and death came to the tribe. They said it was because of Beric, because he had brought down the Anger of the Gods. The warriors of the tribe cast him out. Alone without friends, family or tribe, Beric faces the dangers of the Roman world.

The Silver Branch
Rosemary Sutcliff
ISBN 0 19 271765 2

Violence and intrigue are undermining Rome's influence in Britain. And in the middle of the unrest, Justin and Flavius uncover a plot to overthrow the Emperor. In fear for their lives, they find themselves leading a tattered band of loyalists into the thick of battle in defence of the honour of Rome.

The Lantern Bearers
Rosemary Sutcliff
Winner of the Carnegie Medal
ISBN 0 19 271763 4

The last of the Roman army have set sail and left Britain for ever. They have abandoned the country to civil war and the threat of Saxon invasion. When his home and all he loves are destroyed, Aquila fights to bring some meaning back into his life, and with it the hope of revenge . . .

The Ship That Flew
Hilda Lewis
ISBN 0 19 271768 5

Peter sees the model ship in the shop window and he wants it more than anything else on earth. But it is no ordinary model. The ship takes Peter and his brother and sisters on magical flights, wherever they ask to go. They fly around the world and back into the past. But how long can you keep a ship that is worth everything in the world, and a bit over . . . ?

Minnow on the Say
Philippa Pearce
ISBN 0 19 271778 2

David couldn't believe his eyes. Wedged by the landing stage at the bottom of the garden was a canoe. The *Minnow*. David traces the canoe's owner, Adam, and they begin a summer of adventures. The *Minnow* takes them on a treasure hunt along the river. But they are not the only people looking for treasure, and soon they are caught in a race against time . . .

Tom's Midnight Garden
Philippa Pearce
ISBN 0 19 271793 6 (hardback)
ISBN 0 19 271777 4 (paperback)
Winner of the Carnegie Medal

Tom has to spend the summer at his aunt's and it seems as if
nothing good will ever happen again. Then he hears the
grandfather clock strike thirteen—and everything changes.
Outside the door is a garden—a garden that shouldn't exist.
Are the children there ghosts—or is it Tom who is the ghost?

A Little Lower than the Angels
Geraldine McCaughrean
ISBN 0 19 271780 4
Winner of the Whitbread Children's Novel Award

Gabriel has no idea what the future will hold when he runs
away from his apprenticeship with the bad-tempered
stonemason. But God Himself, in the shape of playmaster
Garvey, has plans for him. He wants Gabriel for his angel . . .
But will Gabriel's new life with the travelling players be any
more secure? In a world of illusion, people are not always what
they seem. Least of all Gabriel.

A Pack of Lies

Geraldine McCaughrean

ISBN 0 19 271788 X

Winner of the Carnegie Medal and the Guardian Children's Fiction Award

Ailsa's life is turned upside down when a strange man moves into her mother's antique shop. He keeps the customers spellbound with his outrageous stories—adventure, horror, romance, mystery—but Ailsa doesn't believe a word. It's all just a pack of lies . . .

Brother in the Land

Robert Swindells

ISBN 0 19 271785 5

Danny's life will never be the same again. He is one of the unlucky ones. A survivor. One of those who have come through a nuclear holocaust alive. He records the sights and events around him, all the time struggling to keep himself and his brother alive.

Flambards

K. M. Peyton

ISBN 0 19 271783 9

Twelve-year-old Christina is sent to live in a decaying old mansion with her fierce uncle and his two sons. She soon discovers a passion for horses and riding, but she has to become part of a strange family. This brooding household is divided by emotional undercurrents and cruelty . . .

This is the first book in the award-winning Flambards series.

The Edge of the Cloud

K. M. Peyton

ISBN 0 19 271782 0

Winner of the Carnegie Medal

Christina and Will have run away together, leaving the tense
atmosphere of Flambards behind. Will is determined to fly one
of the new aeroplanes that are all the rage now, in the early
years of the twentieth century, while Christina finds that people
frown on a young girl working for a living. Worst of all,
Christina realizes that with Will, she will always come second
to his passion for machines.

This is the second book in the Flambards series.

Flambards in Summer

K. M. Peyton

ISBN 0 19 271781 2

Widowed during the First World War, Christina decides to
return to Flambards, the forbidding home of her childhood.
She finds the house is buried in ivy, the paddocks are a jungle,
and the once busy stables are deserted and desolate. So
Christina sets herself the task of turning it into a successful
farm. Together Christina and Dick, the young groom who first
taught her to ride, set about restoring Flambards to its former
glory. But history returns to haunt them . . .

This is the third book in the Flambards series.

Flambards Divided

K. M. Peyton

ISBN 0 19 271787 1

The old ivy-covered house of Flambards has seen many changes since Christina first arrived as a girl of twelve. With the First World War coming to an end, Christina feels the time has come to leave the past behind and look to the future with Dick, the former groom in the stables. But the local gentry refuse to accept Dick into their society and when Major Mark Russell returns from the war in France, Christina finds her feelings divided between these two very different men in her life.

This is the final book in the Flambards series.

Wolf

Gillian Cross

ISBN 0 19 271784 7

Winner of the Carnegie Medal

Cassy hears sinister footsteps in the middle of the night. Suddenly she is packed off to stay with her beautiful feckless mother. There is no explanation. Something has gone frighteningly wrong.

Danger is coming after Cassy. And behind it lurks the dark wolf-shape that seems to slink into everything.

Even her dreams.

The Great Elephant Chase
Gillian Cross
ISBN 0 19 271786 3
Winner of The Smarties Prize and the Whitbread Children's
Novel Award

The elephant changed their lives for ever. Because of the
elephant, Tad and Cissie become entangled in a chase across
America, by train, by flatboat and steam boat. Close behind is
Hannibal Jackson, who is determined to have the elephant for
himself. And how do you hide an enormous Indian elephant?

The Hounds of the Morrigan
Pat O'Shea
ISBN 0 19 271773 1

The Great Queen, the Morrigan, is coming from the West,
bringing destruction to the world. Only two children can stop
her. At times their task seems impossible, and danger is
always present. But they are guided in their quest by an
unforgettable collection of humorous and joyful characters.

But all the time the Morrigan's hounds are trailing them . . .

The Gauntlet
Ronald Welch
ISBN 0 19 271762 6

Stumbling upon the old gauntlet is just the start of an amazing
adventure for Peter. Suddenly he finds himself in the
fourteenth century, in a world of castles, feasts and battles,
where death and danger are always around the corner. Peter
quickly learns to hawk, shoot a longbow, and fight with the
best of them, before facing up to his biggest challenge. Can
Peter escape from the besieged castle and return to his own
time, or will he be another casualty of war himself?

The Piemakers
Helen Cresswell
ISBN 0 19 271809 6

Arthy, Jem and Gravella Roller are the finest pie-makers in
Danby Dale, famed for their perfect pastry and fantastic
fillings. So when they're asked to make a special pie for the
king, which will feed two hundred people, the Rollers are
thrown into a frenzy of excited preparations. This will be the
best ever Danby Dale pie! But unfortunately, wicked Uncle
Crispin, a rival pie-maker, has different plans for the Rollers'
pie . . . plans that include an extra-large helping of pepper . . .

This funny, charming story was Helen Cresswell's first
children's book, and was nominated for the Carnegie Medal.

Jack Holborn
Leon Garfield
ISBN 0 19 271808 8

An action-packed pirate story, with bloodcurdling deaths,
terrifying ghosts, and adventures galore on the high seas.
Orphan Jack Holborn stows away on a ship, little guessing the
dangers and excitement that lie on his journey ahead. Before
long, he finds himself caught up in the middle of a mystery
surrounding his long-lost mother, but before he can discover
the truth, he has to survive the quest through an eerie African
jungle for a famous diamond, worth more than Jack's wildest
dreams.

Mr Corbett's Ghost
Leon Garfield
ISBN 0 19 271810 X

A brilliant collection of three short stories from a master story-
teller, who will keep you turning the pages until the very end.
The chilling title story tells of a young apprentice who makes a
pact with a strange old man one New Year's Eve to rid the
world of Mr Corbett, his cruel employer. Sure enough, Mr
Corbett meets an untimely death, but the tables turn on the
terrified apprentice who finds himself cursed with the ghost of
the man he hated most in the world . . .

Gumble's Yard

John Rowe Townsend

ISBN 0 19 271821 5

Kevin and Sandra have to get away from the house so, with their two young cousins, they gather up all their belongings and make for Gumble's Yard, the deserted row of cottages by the canal.

But the cottages don't appear to be as empty as they first thought—strange people are coming and going from one of the other cottages, mysterious boxes keep arriving, and eventually they find themselves caught in the middle of a dangerous chain of events.

The Intruder

John Rowe Townsend

ISBN 0 19 271820 7

There was something weird about the stranger, something that Arnold didn't like. He made him feel uneasy and suspicious. Always poking his nose in where it wasn't wanted and winding Arnold up. All Arnold wanted was for him to go away and leave him alone but there was only one way he could stop him . . .